TANTE EVA

Nominations due: March 1, 2021
http://bit.ly/SohoPressIN

Nominations due: April 1, 2021
http://bit.ly/SohoPressLR

TANTE EVA

PAULA BOMER

SOHO

beggars and immigrants filling them. Fires broke out with some regularity. She put her bag down and fumbled with her keys. She was shaking fairly badly, finding it difficult to get the key in the lock. The elevator was broken, this she knew, and once in, she walked the ten flights very slowly. Thank goodness for the support hose. She used to travel to the West to buy them. Her legs were thick and swollen and throbbing, just from an hour or so of walking. Some days were harder than others. Some days, she didn't even notice her legs. Some days her legs felt fine, when she was high and happy and when Hansi was waiting outside.

She saw her neighbor Gabi's daughter on the way in. *"Hallo,"* the girl said, standing outside her half-open door. A nice girl, maybe eighteen, but still living with her mother and taking care of her. She had values. Family values. She was devoted. *"Hallo, Krista,"* Eva said.

"Kann ich Dir helfen?" she asked. So many pretty things about her, thought Eva. Long, thick hair, like so many young girls, not aware of how it'll thin. High breasts, cheekbones and a mouth like a pink cushion.

"Danke," Eva said, and Krista took her bags and her keys and let her in to the apartment. If *her* daughter couldn't help her, she may as well borrow her neighbor's. Krista seemed to enjoy helping her. She had a heart. Eva assumed it was also nice to get out of her mother's apartment, to have a break from tending to her mother's every need. The poor woman. She'd been sick for so long.

beggars and immigrants filling them. Fires broke out with some regularity. She put her bag down and fumbled with her keys. She was shaking fairly badly, finding it difficult to get the key in the lock. The elevator was broken, this she knew, and once in, she walked the ten flights very slowly. Thank goodness for the support hose. She used to travel to the West to buy them. Her legs were thick and swollen and throbbing, just from an hour or so of walking. Some days were harder than others. Some days, she didn't even notice her legs. Some days her legs felt fine, when she was high and happy and when Hansi was waiting outside.

She saw her neighbor Gabi's daughter on the way in. *"Hallo,"* the girl said, standing outside her half-open door. A nice girl, maybe eighteen, but still living with her mother and taking care of her. She had values. Family values. She was devoted. *"Hallo, Krista,"* Eva said.

"Kann ich Dir helfen?" she asked. So many pretty things about her, thought Eva. Long, thick hair, like so many young girls, not aware of how it'll thin. High breasts, cheekbones and a mouth like a pink cushion.

"Danke," Eva said, and Krista took her bags and her keys and let her in to the apartment. If *her* daughter couldn't help her, she may as well borrow her neighbor's. Krista seemed to enjoy helping her. She had a heart. Eva assumed it was also nice to get out of her mother's apartment, to have a break from tending to her mother's every need. The poor woman. She'd been sick for so long.

• • •

She tried to reason with herself, to calm herself. They only hurt the Turks and the Arabs and the Africans, of whom there were so many now that the Wall was down. They weren't crazy about some of the Slavs, either, the darker ones. When eastern Germany had been East Germany, she was never scared, not once. There was no crime. There were no skinheads, not visibly at least.

Now, well, now it was very different. It wasn't the city she'd moved to decades ago. And even then, she moved here because of Hugo, her husband. But it was her home now. It had been for a long time. She still had her Austrian passport. Her brother lived in Vienna and had for years told her to move there. She couldn't. For one, she couldn't leave her lover, Hansi. Never could she leave him. She loved her siblings—her brother in Vienna, her sister in America—but she didn't want to move. She just wanted the old GDR back. And she wanted her Hansi, too, even though he was married, even though he hid things from her. She knew he hid things from her to protect her. But sometimes she wanted to know him better, to know everything about him. If he only had more time for her. If only he would leave that woman. Marry *her*. When she caught herself thinking this way, she tried to reason with herself. One thought was, *in time*. In time, they would be together.

Her building stretched up high above her. All around were empty lots, half-torn-down buildings, and squatters and even though she tried to convince herself they wouldn't hurt *her*. She was very Aryan. Wasn't that what they worshipped? Blonde, blue-eyed people—the master race? Why menace *her*? She tried walking more quickly, something she was sure they noticed. She looked down at the sidewalk, avoiding their gaze. She sped up a bit, ashamed, ashamed of her fear. Fear and anger, how they go together, what twins they are. The smallest of the group—shorter than her, the short ones always had to prove themselves—started following her. He was to the left of her now, imitating her awkward gait. He smelled like alcohol. He brandished his bottle of beer like a weapon. Out of the corner of her eye, she noticed his leather jacket, his tattered jeans, his black boots. A swastika tattoo on his neck. It wasn't the first time she'd seen any of them, and yet she couldn't help noticing more details each time. When one of them got a new tattoo, when they were so high they just slouched sitting with their backs against the abandoned corner building, when one had a black eye. And she knew some of their names at this point. The ringleader was Johann.

"*Kann ich Ihnen helfen, Fräulein?*" he asked, making a bowing motion at her.

"*Nein danke,*" she said. She looked at him, trying to avoid his eyes, but they caught. Something about his face made her shudder—the wide nose, the weak chin, the hanging lips. He looked like someone she once knew. Was he one of her daughter's old classmates? What happened to people?

Finally, he was behind her.

CHAPTER 1

It was dark even though it was only four thirty in the afternoon. That's how it was in November. Eva walked the five blocks from the shopping district to her apartment building, an immensely tall, white building, constructed in the 1960s. In any other country it would have been a housing project, but in East Berlin at the time it was built, everyone—well, almost everyone—lived in buildings like hers. Now, her area had become a sort of slum. She walked slowly, the support hose chafing her thighs. She had varicose veins and was overweight, and the hose helped, for the most part. She passed a group of skinheads standing on the corner. *"Guten Abend, Fräulein,"* one said in a deep, joking voice. Laughter broke out. There were three of them this afternoon, smoking cigarettes, bottles of beer in their hands. One was clearly the ringleader, the one who had greeted her. He was mocking her; she wasn't stupid. They were probably in their twenties, but they looked ancient—translucent skin, a glowing red emanating from underneath. She knew what that was—the drink. Often she thought, where are their mothers?

She had in mind to greet them back, but she was afraid,

TANTE EVA

I hear a lot of people saying
Socialism—well all right,
But what they're pulling on us here
It isn't worth a light!
I see a lot of people clenching
Buried fists in mackintoshes.
Dog-ends hang cold from their lips,
And in their hearts are ashes.
—Wolf Biermann

The [GDR] was the anti-fascist phoenix that rose from
the ashes of the Nazi inferno.
—Unknown East German

For my mother, again. And everything is always for my sons.

Published by
Soho Press, Inc.
227 W 17th Street
New York, NY 10011

Library of Congress Cataloging-in-Publication Data

Bomer, Paula, author.
Tante Eva / Paula Bomer.

ISBN 978-1-641292-221-6
eISBN 978-1-64129-223-8

PS3602.O65496 T36 2021 | DDC 813'.6—dc23
LC record available at https://lccn.loc.gov/2020053038

Interior design by Janine Agro, Soho Press, Inc.

Printed in the United States of America

10 9 8 7 6 5 4 3 2 1

TANTE EVA

PAULA BOMER

SOHO

· · ·

After holding the door for Eva, Krista came in and locked the door behind them. She set down the canvas bag with milk, cheese, and coffee, as well as the sleeping pills. Eva didn't hide anything from Krista at this point. Krista knew about the pills. God knows what her mother was on. She began laying out everything on the counter for Eva, hanging the bag on a hook next to the sink.

"*Du bist so lieb, Krista,*" Eva said.

"*Ach, das ist doch nichts,*" Krista said and sat down on the hard-backed wooden chair at the small table against the wall. "*Wie geht's? Was machen deine Beine?*"

Eva sat on her twin bed, a cot really, and rubbed her legs. She wanted to take off her hose. They were constricting and she was ready to be rid of them, even though they were so helpful. As close as she felt to Krista, she'd never undressed in front of her. "*Nicht so gut heute, wenn ich ehrlich bin,*" she said.

"*Das tut mir leid, Eva,*" Krista said, and looked at her with a piercing sort of warmth, a look new to Eva.

"*Ich könnte sie massieren,*" Krista offered.

Eva was taken slightly aback. This was new. She'd never offered to rub her legs before. She always inquired as to how Eva's legs were; she knew of Eva's pain. Eva knew that Krista changed her mother's bedpans, bathed her, did everything for her. Rubbing her legs was nothing in comparison, perhaps.

"*Wirklich?*" Eva asked.

"*Hier, lass mich mal,*" Krista said, and knelt on the cheap blue rug at the side of Eva's bed. Eva watched as Krista removed first her shoes, untying them carefully, setting them, lined up, next to her. They were good shoes; they weren't leather, they were synthetic, but they had cushioned supporting soles. Then, Krista, determined, began pulling down Eva's stockings. Eva, to her great discomfort, felt a second of arousal, and her face went red.

"Krista," she said, "*lass mich.*" She tried to stand. Krista, hands on Eva's thighs, pulled them down and off swiftly, much more quickly and less painfully then when Eva did it herself.

There was a whiff of stink in the air, like sour milk. Eva's flesh, her feet. Now the two women looked at each other as Krista began to massage Eva's thighs. Eva stared into Krista's gray eyes. Then she looked down at her own legs—blotchy, but mostly pale with a slight olive undertone. Her sister claimed their ancestors had been raped by Genghis Khan, which is why they weren't totally fair skinned. Rivers of veins under the flesh, rising at points, then fading deep into her body. Krista's hands were long fingered and she slightly pinched when she dug into Eva's thighs. She looked at the top of Krista's head, a middle part down her visibly oily hair. The scalp that showed had white flakes, and Eva could smell her too, not just herself.

She closed her eyes. A vision of washing her younger sister's hair in Leoben, after her mother died and she became the caregiver. Wrapping her naked six-year-old body in a towel, rubbing her dry, hairless vagina, her tears. "*Nicht so doll,*" she'd cry. And Eva, overwhelmed, saying, *"Halt die Klappe!"* Eva then would brush her tangled hair and Liezel would try not to cry, saying, *"Das tut weh."* Eva ripped through, saying nothing, yanking harder as she braided her hair, hoping it hurt her.

"Zu doll?" Krista asked, a bit of perspiration on her upper lip, above that pink cushion mouth.

"Nein, nein," Eva said. It was slightly too hard, but she wasn't going to look a gift horse in the mouth. She leaned back against the wall. Krista stopped for a minute to put the one pillow on the bed behind Eva's back.

"Du bist ein Engel," Eva said quietly, and Krista rubbed and rubbed, from her thighs down to her feet, ending by rubbing each toe, one at a time.

After Krista left, Eva sat there on her bed and felt how smoothly her breath came and went. She closed her eyes and thought about how soon she could take her night pill. Since she'd stopped working as a nurse, she worried about getting her prescriptions filled. But there had been no problems. She took stimulants in the morning and often at lunch, sleeping pills at night. Six of each of them on a good day, more if she was having a bad day. She knew it was why she trembled. She knew it was why she sometimes saw things late at night, when the blue light of the moon shone into her room, on her bed, next to the only window in her apartment. She knew all this, of course. And so? It was her life. It was how she liked things.

She'd first eat. She had some bread from yesterday; it was

stale, but it would do. She cut it into thick slices and then cut
the cheese, layering it with care on the bread. She sat at the
table. There was a bottle of red wine on the table, and she
poured herself a large water glass full of it. She was home.
As humble as it was—one rectangular room, the small table
against the wall with two chairs, her bed, a wardrobe, and her
record player on a low table with a handful of records stacked
neatly beneath—it was hers.

She would eat in silence tonight. Maybe take an extra sleeping pill or two and then play a record. Yes. That is what she
would do.

The wine was turning to vinegar, but she drank it anyway, using
it to wash down her dinner. She thought about dutiful Krista,
still so attached to her mother. Gabi, Frau Haufmann, was lucky
in that way, although her health problems were endless, and
that was certainly not lucky. Eva had been that way, like Krista,
a devoted caregiver. She wasn't like her sister, knowing from
a very young age that she would leave Leoben, Austria. After
their mother died, Eva took over managing the house. And it
had suited her very well. Those years before her father remarried were, in some ways, the happiest of her life. Of course,
she hadn't always been the best mother figure to her siblings.
She wasn't perfect. But it gave her something—a purpose. And
more than that. It filled the hours of the day. It took away her
choices, and yet, oddly, she never felt so free. There was her
brother, Willi, to look after and her outgoing and determined

sister, Liezel. She was the oldest, Willi had been eleven and Liezel, the fireball, was only six when their mother died.

Eva had been a beautiful young woman. At fifteen, she was a young woman, not a teenager like her daughter at the same age, in a different world, in East Berlin decades later. In Leoben, she was a young woman at fifteen. She dressed in her mother's dirndls—they fit her perfectly—and did all the grocery shopping and kept the accounts and cleaned the house and sang to Liezel, sang to her at night before kissing her goodnight. *Shlaf gut.*

Eva supposed that if she were to interpret her life in the contemporary fashion—as her daughter did, as even Liezel did—she'd be forced to think of herself as someone who had her childhood or adolescence cruelly taken away from her. That this was the root of all her problems. Well, she may not have been a naturally adventurous person, and she may not have been a modern woman, one who takes control of her life, but she always thought for herself. And no matter how hard she tried, she couldn't believe such a facile understanding of a life. She may have felt guilty at the serenity and joy she felt after her mother died. But she knew she loved her mother. She hated watching her suffer at home, then in the hospital, the lupus slowing sucking the life out of her. But once she was gone, once she was dead, Eva was given something, too. She was given a responsibility that suited her. She had been more than eager to shed her childhood. Aren't all children desperate to grow up? And adolescence, well, what is that but a prolonged childhood? Who wants that? Childhood was a cruel, animal stage of life, a life of uncertainty, chaos, and fear. Adults were reasonable. Adulthood made sense.

She had pictures of herself from then. Black-and-white photos, only a few of them. She was healthy and red cheeked, and her hair was thick and blonde. Her eyebrows were thick, too, and dark, and her lips were wide and red, just like her cheeks. She looked nothing like the sullen, skinny teenagers she saw walking the streets of Berlin. Since the Wall came down, they'd become even worse. Even thinner and more unsmiling and cynical. Today, she'd have been thought of as heavy, Eva supposed. But then, she knew she was healthy. They mostly had plenty of food—milk, eggs, sometimes even meat, thanks to their cousin Lois and his farm outside of town. Well, maybe it wasn't quite like that in 1944, but it was still that way in '42. That year, they would go to visit Uncle Lois, and he was so generous with them. But by '44, it was true, they'd outworn their welcome, and they had to stop the visits. Uncle Lois barely had enough for himself and his children by then. Eva didn't begrudge him.

It was all so long ago, but what was Eva to do, except think about the past? She had stopped working as a nurse about four years ago, right before the Wall came down. The changes were coming, she knew, and it was all too much for her. She decided it was a sign for her to quit. She'd done her time, yes. She'd worked as a nurse for most of her adult life. Who knew what would happen to health care? East Germany hadn't been perfect. That had always been hard for her to admit, but she could more easily now that it no longer existed. But at least it had had great health care and education. The best—and for everyone.

She finished her glass of wine and poured another large glass, standing, taking her dish to the sink. Enough of the past. She had Hansi, sort of, her boyfriend of the past ten years. He was getting along with his wife these days and wasn't making much time for her. When he was miserable at home was when Eva was happiest, when her Hans was lonely and needed her. She tried to convince herself he would need her again. That he'd call her again. He always did come back to her eventually. Ten years of back and forth, between her and the wife, Paula. In the early days, when he would return to Paula and their big house outside of the city, after spending a few nights with her, she'd beg. She'd ask him to stay, falling to her knees, and grab his legs. So pathetic. He'd always leave, often slapping her away as she clung to him. Afterward, Eva would feel that her life was over. That he would never call her again. That she should just kill herself. But after ten years, she had more faith in him. Hans loved her, too. He loved two women, and he wasn't the first man to do so, was he? Her husband, Hugo, had loved at least that many when he was alive. He would come back, her Hansi. And she would be waiting for him.

But not tonight, no. No Hansi tonight. A big, thick man, with a brown leather jacket, his head bare, a cigarette between his fingers. The smell of his well-oiled leather and his cigarettes alone would make her dizzy with lust. She knew what other people in her building thought. Hansi gave off an air of menace, so no one said anything, of course. He had worked for the police; this she knew, but not much more. He'd get angry if she prodded, so she stopped prodding a long time ago. Two middle-aged lovers, neither thin, both with plenty of lines on their faces. He was her joy. Her daughter disapproved but had grown used to his presence in her life. Ten years. Thick Hansi and Eva with her bright red, nearly purple, dyed hair, set neatly into a helmet around her often anxious face. Since the Wall came down, there were many more hair dyes available. But Eva had grown used to this particular shade of red. In fact, she was afraid her drugstore would stop carrying it, now that all the French brands were everywhere. The thought of losing her violet-red hair! It would be like losing a breast, she thought.

She hung her dress up in her wardrobe. Then she swallowed her pills with the rest of her wine, and grunting, her joints creaking, got under the blankets. No music tonight. Krista's massage, the pills, the thick slabs of cheese. Soon she'd be free of consciousness, dead to the world. She closed her eyes. Another day gone.

CHAPTER 2

Eva woke around eleven the next morning. It hurt to wake. Her head felt swollen and foggy, and she didn't want to get up. But she couldn't lie there for long; she had to use the bathroom badly. She went into her bathroom—a toilet and bathtub with no sink—and peed. Her head started to pound and burn. How it hurt to stop dreaming. Waking and leaving her dreams was in many ways the hardest part of her day. She had dreamed that Hansi was with her in bed, caressing her, kissing her face. She'd orgasmed in her sleep—that she remembered. There was more, too, but it was a bit vague. There was a house by a lake he had, and they were on a train, passing it. He was pointing it out to her. He was very proud, but frowning. It was dark in the dream, too, like today, as Eva could tell through her one window from the bathroom where she sat on the toilet now, resting before getting up and starting her day. A gloomy day. Maybe rain, maybe snow. In the dream, Hans was saying, "I'll take you there someday." Silly, she thought as she began boiling water to make coffee, her hands trembling, as she swallowed four *Morgen tabletten*. In reality, he had taken her there twice already, once for a a few nights when his wife was in the Soviet Union. Another time just for a night, when Paula was visiting relatives in Poland. In the dream, she was so excited, he was pointing out the house to her, and she'd felt as if she'd never seen it. And in the dream, she was so happy to be with him. She could smell him in her dream—the cigarettes, the leather, the hair pomade he used. In the dream, even though he was frowning, she was happy.

There was a knock on her door. It could only be a few people. She wasn't scared, but she wasn't properly awake, either. *"Moment, Moment,"* Eva called as she put on her robe.

It was Krista, her face clean for a change, but wearing the slightly odorous purple sweater with the sparkles in it that she wore almost every day. It was her favorite sweater, and for some reason, this touched Eva.

"Frau Eva," Krista said, "would you like me to check your mail for you? I'm going downstairs to check ours."

"Danke, Krista, gerne," Eva said. The girl knew it was hard for Eva to take the stairs. Eva fetched her mail key. So kind, Eva thought, trying to get her thoughts straight, away from sleep and dreams, and then the image of Krista rubbing her feet, her oily hair parted so expertly down the middle, the thick white flakes—she had wanted to pick them off her head. Eva shuddered. Perhaps there would be a letter from Hans. Perhaps Paula and he were fighting again and now he'd write to her, telling her where and when to meet him. Although he almost never wrote, he usually just showed up, waiting in the

shadows of the building. But he had written her a few times. She kept the letters. They weren't very telling, but they were from him and they meant the world to her. She knew he had to be careful—he couldn't write how he loved her. He couldn't do that. How long had it been since she'd heard from him? Six months? She didn't even want to think about it.

Eva busied herself with coffee, with washing her face, with teasing a comb through her hair. When Krista returned, she burst through the doorway and said, "It's a letter from America!"

Eva looked at the envelope. The coffee and the pills were working now, and she could think clearly. It wasn't from her sister, Liezel. It was from her niece, Maggie, her sister's daughter. Maggie had lived in West Berlin for a summer in the eighties. She'd studied at the Goethe Institute off the Ku'damm and lived in Kreuzberg, near where Eva's own daughter lived. Eva had gone to visit her a number of times—her Austrian passport allowed this—and Maggie came to visit her in the East, too. She liked this niece. She knew her, unlike Liezel's other daughters, whom she'd never met.

Krista hovered around, excited.

"It's from my niece," she said. "Sit. I'll read it to you, if you'd like."

"Oh, yes. I'd like that. I remember her very well."

One of the times that Maggie had visited Eva, Krista came over. They all drank coffee together and talked. Krista had been so delighted to practice her English, and with a real

American, too. It was the first time Krista had met someone from the West. Then, six years ago, it was a very special thing. Americans rarely came to East Germany.

"*Die Karte ist auf Englisch,*" Eva said. Krista sat upright, her scratched glasses perched on her nose.

"*Wunderbar!*" said the girl.

"Would you like to read it to me?" Eva then asked. "Your English is better than mine. Read it to me in English, and then maybe I'll ask you to explain to me things in German I don't understand, okay?"

"*Ja, kein Problem,*" Krista said and took the letter from Eva. Eva observed Krista closely, how she gripped the paper unnecessarily hard, how she held it so close to her face, undoubtedly because her glasses were so old and scratched—but also out of excitement. She read at a nice even pace, not slowly. Her English was so good. Eva thought of how hard she must study. Eva wanted to interrupt but she let the girl read straight through. She looked up at Eva once, but otherwise kept her eyes on the thin airmail paper, see-through thin, like an onion skin.

Dear Tante Eva,

How are you? It has been so long since I've been in touch and I'm sorry. But I'm sure you understand how our daily lives can take over and then suddenly, years have gone by. I finished with college just a few weeks ago. I went to school in Boston, to Boston University, where

I studied political science. I am nervous that school is over and not quite sure what to do with myself. My mother thinks I should apply to graduate schools right away, but I am thinking of traveling some first, and maybe even getting a job and working for a while before going back to school. I want to live in the real world and experience things before going to university again. I realize how fortunate I am to have these choices—most people don't have the choices and privileges I have, but I think I'd be better at whatever I choose to do in life if I spend some time working. Sometimes, I think I may want to study nursing, like you. Maybe that sounds strange to you—political science and nursing. The connection between the two for me is that I'd like to practice nursing in a foreign country, maybe with Doctors Without Borders—have you heard of them?—or another relief agency.

My mother told me you stopped working recently. How is that going? And the Wall coming down? I'm sure it's much easier to see your daughter, Elena. I think about you and how kind you were to me when I was in Berlin. I enjoyed that summer immensely.

In fact, I was thinking of returning. Fairly certain I can make it happen. And perhaps getting a job, and maybe even taking some courses at a university in Berlin. My German is still quite good—I belonged to a German-speaking club while in college.

At school, I studied with a man named Howard Zinn. You would like him, Tante Eva. Not all Americans are capitalists. And I read many books by Noam Chomsky. Have you heard of him? He is a linguist and a political activist. I was very moved by both of these men—they taught me a lot about the injustices of capitalism and the "free" world. I just now am reading about Dorothy Day, another American political activist you would like. She's a Catholic, too! Just like you and Mom were, growing up in Austria.

I worry about you, now that your country has changed. Or do you feel like it is gone altogether?

One good thing—I am fairly certain you'll get this letter! And it won't take three months and it won't have been opened and read by someone else! But perhaps that is little comfort to you.

I also have met a man, whom I love very much. He believes in the things that I do. He may come with me to Berlin. He doesn't know any German, but he's very bright—in fact, he's brilliant in my estimation—and he would learn quickly. You would like him, Tante Eva. My mother doesn't, as you can imagine.

Anyway, I will keep you updated of my plans. I want so much to see you. I hope you are well.

Viele Busserl,
Maggie

Krista handed the letter back to Eva. She normally wasn't an excitable girl, but this was something special, and she was noticeably changed. Hope of a future joy, thought Eva, how it can lead to a piercing disappointment! Then Eva shook off that thought.

"Krista, wie gut du Englisch liest!" she said. *"Ich bin wirklich beindruckt."*

"Danke," Krista said. *"Ich kann dir gerne helfen, auf Englisch zurück zu schreiben."*

Eva probably could write it on her own, but why not let the girl help her?

"That would be wonderful. When do you think you'd be able to help me?"

"This evening, after school?"

"Okay, bis dann," Eva said, *"um vier?"*

"Five o'clock would be better, if that's okay," Krista said, getting up, not looking at Eva. "I have to take care of my mother first."

"Of course," Eva said. "It's been too long since I've visited her. I'm ashamed. I should come by sometime."

"It's okay, Eva. You have your bad legs, and my mother—honestly, it's exhausting for her to have visitors. But yes, we'll schedule something." Krista started to leave, and then turned, *"Danke, Eva,"* she said, "for letting me read the letter to you. I'm excited to see Maggie again, if that would be possible."

"Selbstverständlich!" said Eva, "Of course. We'll have dinner together when she comes. It will be my treat."

Eva thought she saw some color come to Krista's pale face. As the girl closed the door behind her, Eva sat there holding the letter, looking at Maggie's lovely handwriting. It was a surprise and it wasn't a surprise at the same time. She folded the letter very carefully. She'd have to buy stamps today. She still had paper and envelopes. She went to her wardrobe and opened a shallow drawer, putting the letter in it, the drawer of special correspondence. Letters from Hansi, letters that were meaningful, from her brother, from her sister. It was a drawer full of proof of people who had once loved her. She rarely reread any of the letters. It was too emotional. It was almost proof of her own existence. Maggie was most likely coming to see her, in person—something that you can't put in a drawer.

CHAPTER 3

She more than enjoyed this niece's interest in her. She enjoyed the fact that Liezel's daughter liked her better than she liked her own mother. *Schadenfreude* toward her own sister. It shamed Eva. She didn't wish bad things upon Liezel, did she? She couldn't want her sister to suffer, could she? There had been times when she knew Liezel had suffered, and it broke her heart. When Liezel's husband, Fred, had a nervous break-down, from which he never quite recovered. That had been a very rough time in Liezel's life, and she had written Eva a few letters. She had even called once. When Hugo was alive, they'd had a telephone. Now Eva used the phone in the hallway. That was fine with her. She didn't need her own phone anymore.

And there was their mother's death. The gruesomeness of it. Something she tried and managed, mostly, to never think about. She had no say in that matter.

Maggie reminded Eva of her Liezel, but she didn't say that to Maggie. That was most likely why they didn't get along—both too headstrong for their own good, full of crazy opinions, not very good listeners. But Liezel knew that about her daughter. Even when Maggie was a little girl, five or six, Liezel would say, "She's a real handful—so obstinate, and loud, too."

Eva had only seen pictures of Maggie as a little girl. She didn't meet her until that summer she studied in Berlin. In the pictures, she looked nothing like Liezel. Liezel would write to Eva, "She looks just like you." And there in the picture of her niece, Eva would see herself and her long dead mother. The turned-up nose, the blonde hair, the thick eyebrows, the round face. Liezel was dark and Slavic looking—thick-lipped, slightly wide-nosed—like their father. And Eva's own daughter, Elena, looked like her dead husband, Hugo, with nearly black hair, profoundly dark eyes, and a prominent, narrow nose.

It was almost as if Maggie were hers, in some way. That's how Eva felt when she saw those pictures and also during those visits in Berlin in the eighties. That Maggie belonged to her some-how. That she'd been born into the wrong family. And Maggie felt that way, too. Sometimes, Eva thought, God sends you gifts. To Eva, Maggie felt like a gift from God, a God who often was unkind, as anyone who's read the Bible knows. Eva knew suffer-ing, so when something miraculous came along—a niece who was more like an angel, a twin in a different time, as if her own youth were given a new chance at life—she knew to be grateful.

So, she reasoned with herself, it wasn't just Schadenfreude, her enjoyment of Maggie's affection. The way she looked, and then later, her political views. She was part of a plan that God had. An act of grace? Eva believed in God, very much. When she married Hugo, an atheist Jew, she more or less abandoned the Catholic Church, but not God. Never did she abandon God. Indeed, she saw His work regularly, saw His hand pass over things. Mostly at night, playing her records—a collection of Negro spirituals and blues recordings that she acquired when Hugo was alive. She'd had access to such things when they weren't available in the GDR. Hugo had been a beloved photographer, part of the intelligentsia. That was why they had the house—they both knew that—and the ability to get records from the US. Liezel didn't send them. If she had tried, they wouldn't have gotten to Eva.

Not that Liezel would have. She was perhaps kind, but not generous. When she left Austria for France and met her American husband, also a student there, and then moved to America, she had abandoned more than the Catholic Church. She abandoned God. Like Hugo. Atheists. Eva had loved Hugo like no one else. Hans was her lover, but Hugo had been the love of her life. She never held his atheism against him. She didn't even think about it. He was who he was—a Jew who survived World War II, who survived the camps. How could he not be touched by God? It didn't matter what he believed. God believed in him. That's what mattered.

But Liezel was different. Her, Eva judged. She actively let go of so much, but she wasn't as blessed as Hugo, and so, in Eva's mind, it was a horrible thing. She let go of God, she let go of socialism, and she moved to the country that was responsible for the poverty and starvation of so many. America! And Liezel used to invite Eva to visit! Never would she set foot in that country, never. Where blacks had been slaves, traded like cattle. Where education and health care were only for the rich. Where so few lived like kings and the majority lived in squalor. They had seen movies, Hugo and Eva and all of their acquaintances, of the slums of Chicago. These were movies played often in East Germany, at the state-owned cinemas. Of the hungry and malformed living in West Virginia, dying in coal mines. Liezel was different from Hugo, despite their atheism. Liezel had let go of so much that she'd become almost cynical, definitely selfish, concerned only with herself like a good capitalist, whereas Hugo, more than anyone Eva knew, believed in the possibility of a better, safer world, where justice and integrity could be had by all.

When Liezel was a little girl, Eva was her whole world. Eva was a decade older, and Liezel worshipped her. She wanted to have blonde hair like Eva's and blue eyes like Eva's. She'd pull at her dark hair and look so sad. *"I möchte aussehen wie du,"* she'd say, in her sweet little girl voice and her large dark eyes were sad like a calf's.

Liezel was Eva's "first daughter." When her own daughter arrived, years later, it didn't affect her as it did some new mothers. She felt she'd done it all before. She worried that this had caused her problems with Elena, that Elena knew she wasn't really her first child, her first maternal love.

She remembered very well when her mother brought Liezel home from the hospital. The war hadn't really affected their part of Austria yet, at least not in any way that Eva was aware of. Their mother and father, though not without problems, she guessed, seemed very much in love. He was a tailor, and she worked hard to take care of their home and the children. When Liezel was born, Eva began helping more than ever around the house. She learned how to change diapers and gave baby Liezel baths. She fed her food that she ground herself in a baby-food grinder, taking the scraps she kept after preparing the meals for her brother and father, and putting them all together in the hand grinder, swinging the arm of the grinder around and around in circles, until the food was mush. And she'd hold her baby sister's sweet, milky-sour flesh against her own and sing to her, rocking her gently, until she'd fall asleep. She often watched her mother breastfeed with envy. How she loved her little baby sister. How she'd wished she were *her* baby.

Her mother was thirty then, still young and still healthy, before the lupus attacked her. It was before the war affected them. It was a time of innocence, in Eva's mind. A time of hope.

That time disappeared rapidly.

Sometimes she wondered if her mother got sick because of the war. And her father, Franz Stiller, stupidly volunteering near the end of it. On a drunken bet, he volunteered. Eva remembered the argument. Her mother crying, yelling. Her father rough and domineering, as he often was. He was too old—much older than their mother—and too nearsighted to be drafted. And he hated the Nazis. He hated them for killing his sister, who'd suffered from epilepsy. Eva hadn't known her aunt very well. But her father knew when they took her to the hospital, before the war even started, that she wasn't coming back. The idiots, the mongoloids, the homosexuals, all the many varieties of the handicapped. They all went first. But her father was the sort of man who became stupid when he was drunk—and the sort of man who never backed out of any bet he made. Pride, the sin of Lucifer himself.

Just like that—and he was gone. Willi missed him the most. He became unmanageable. And so, they made him stay out until supper, and then again, until bedtime. *"Raus! Raus mit dir!"* she remembered her mother yelling. And Eva, too, would yell that at him, if he came home to sit around, sullen and angry and throwing things. *Raus!*

In her own marriage, she didn't know who was the crueler. It always appeared that way from the outside, that one is crueler than the other, but often it's the opposite in private. Behind closed doors, the one who seems kinder, the one who appears to be the victim, may be the most insidious, the most vicious.

A week after she received the letter, the phone rang in the hall. Most everyone had their own phone, but not Eva nor Krista and her mother. Eva was home and heard it. The walls in the building were made from cheap particle board—everyone could hear everything. Eva walked down the hall and answered it. It was her daughter, Elena.

"*Hallo, Mutti,*" she said.

"*Hallo, Elena, Liebchen, was ist los?*"

Her daughter did not call often. She often thought, despite their distance, that they were close enough. They were in each other's lives, weren't they? Elena had moved to the West in her late teens and resented her mother for bringing her up in the GDR. To leave, she had to defect, to abandon the country and all she knew. Afterward, she had been forbidden to return. This was only because Elena had been foolish enough to join the Party. If she hadn't been such an enthusiastic Communist in her teens, they would have been much more lenient on her, but when a Party member left, it was a betrayal that caused a casting out. It had been a harsh time. In some ways, it was after Hugo died that the resentment began. Elena's resentment of her changed shapes and forms—for not providing her a father, as if it were Eva's fault he died. Perhaps, for not giving them a life in the West— but it was all the same to Eva. Blaming. Self-pitying. Eva had loved her. Had she loved her enough? She thought so. She loved being a mother. She loved being the mother of Hugo's daughter. But Elena had become a modern girl, a girl who perhaps always belonged in the West—selfish and complaining. Perhaps everyone is a product of their time, she reasoned. We are what we are. At some point, a mother has to let go.

"Did you get a letter from Maggie?"

"Yes, I did. "

"*Ich auch. Wie toll*, that she's probably coming to visit, no?"

"*Genau*, I'm looking forward to it. She hasn't been here since the Wall came down."

"*Ja, ich weiss*. I wonder if she'll like it better, like everyone else in the world except you."

Eva knew there would be a jab. There rarely was a conversation without some sort of insult, some confrontation. She stayed silent.

"*Willst du heute vielleicht vorbeikommen?*" Elena then asked, with a kindness in her voice. Elena could be unkind, but she knew it at least; sometimes, she felt bad, felt contrite. "Come by. I'll take you out to lunch."

"Really? That would be nice," said Eva.

"Yes! Come."

The neighborhood where Elena lived had changed much in the past few years. Before the Wall came down, Kreuzberg was all Turks and a handful of crazy hippie artists like her daughter. It had been an immigrant neighborhood—run down, with crumbling buildings that had once been beautiful but had not been kept up. Small, gilded buildings—not the high rises built after the war, not like the building she lived in. They had "character," or what the Soviets would think of as unnecessary decorative aspects. The neighborhood was known for having a lot of crime, and it still did, but much

less. Most of the crime had moved east, to where Eva lived, as
had the immigrants. Now Kreuzberg was somewhat fashion-
able. Cafés, hip clothing stores, renovation after renovation.
Middle-class families with artistic leanings moved in and took
over. Elena hated it. She found it "bougie." But she wasn't
stupid enough to give up her great three-bedroom apartment, overlooking a canal. And she loved the cafés, although
she didn't care to say so.

Eva, on the other hand, flat out loved Kreuzberg. She
loved how alive it felt. She loved the clothing stores, in particular. The clothes young people made! Some of it was too
crazy for her—pants cut so low they showed the crack of your
bottom and so long they dragged along the ground, T-shirts
with ripped sleeves and safety pins and naked women painted
on them. Yes, they were all too much, but she enjoyed looking at them anyway. Sometimes she found a scarf or a hat
that she'd buy for herself. She loved clothes. She loved the
way they could grab attention, bring attention to oneself.
She loved clothes that made her feel pretty.

The door to Elena's building was open and Eva walked
up one flight and knocked. Elena answered, a cigarette in
one hand and a beer in the other. She lived on beer and cigarettes, and it showed. She was thin and haggard and wore the
same blue jeans every day. Yet she seemed younger than her
nearly thirty years. She was a perpetual child. She goofed off,
she acted out, she didn't wear makeup or care about anything
but her art and her friends. She wasn't a bad person. But she

confounded Eva. She could have been a beautiful woman,
but she chose not to be. She could have had a job in a university teaching art, but instead she worked in a pub, serving
beers and mopping floors. She embodied underachievement,
and sometimes it made Eva ache.

"Hallo, Mutti!"

"Hallo, hallo, Liebchen."

They kissed, straight on the lips, a tradition from Eva's
Austrian peasant roots, and Eva followed her daughter into
her apartment. It was true, she was envious. But then, she
knew she didn't really need this sort of space. When Elena
had moved here, it was worth nothing. And now it was worth
a fortune. But Elena paid very little for the place because
it was rent stabilized. The sun was trying to shine today,
through the thick November air. Elena's windows let the
light in. Eva sat on the only chair in the room that was of
normal height—everything else was pillowy and low to the
ground and would make her knee-length skirt awkward.

"Willst du ein Bier, Mutti?"

"Ja, gerne, warum nicht?" Eva was not a big beer drinker,
but she was fairly certain that was all Elena had in the house.
Beer made her sleepy, but she'd be fine. She'd take an extra
stimulant later, or take a nap.

"I have some new records that I thought you'd like. I can
even give you one, as a present. How's that? I found them
cheap. They're used. A bit scratched up. But it's the blues,
the real thing. You'll love them." It was something they had

in common, music. It was something they both liked very much and liked about each other.

Elena walked over to her player, a new-looking, slick, black machine. Again, Eva felt the envy rise in her. Elena put on a record and brought over the sleeves and covers for Eva to look at. Nina Simone started singing. Elena sat near her mother, on an enormous pillow with a pink, paisley cover.

Nina sang, "I loves you Porgy. / Don't let him take me. / Don't let him handle me . . ."

Oh, what gorgeous suffering. Eva's eyes filled. The music of God. Of God's people suffering. She closed her eyes and listened. But the wetness dripped on her cheeks.

"Ah, Mutti, komm mir jetzt bitte nicht so komisch, so krass drauf, bitte," Elena said, laughing.

"Laugh at me," Eva said. "You know you cry when you listen to this music. You just do it when you are alone. I don't have such control." She said, wiping her eyes. Would Elena give her this one? Should she ask, or wait and see what happened? She would wait. Wait and see. Nina Simone sang, and Eva closed her eyes. There was hope, too, and beauty, of course. It wasn't just suffering.

"So your dear niece is coming!" Elena said.

"Yes, but we don't know when. But yes. You like her too, no? I remember you two hanging out at pubs together, talking about art."

"Yeah, that was fun. But now I gather she is a serious political scientist, whatever that means."

"She's just a young girl, fresh out of university."

"Yes, but you know how I hate politics. And I think she wants to stay here. And this time, she doesn't know for how long."

"Let her stay for a while. She'll find her own place quickly enough. She's not a freeloader. She's very resourceful. You could use the money, too, if you wanted to ask her to pay some of the rent. And give her some time. She'll grow to hate politics too, like any sane person."

They both laughed at this, again, a thing they had in common. The general distrust of politics. Not that they didn't have ideas.

"Well, what if she's not sane?" asked Elena.

Eva thought about that for a minute. She could very well not be sane. She wouldn't be alone in the family. Eva often thought that Elena could be a depressive. Like her Hugo. Like her father, maybe. "Well, we can't do anything about that, now can we?"

"Ah, Mutti, always with the practical response. What can we ever do? Nothing! Nothing about anything!" Elena downed her beer and belched loudly. "Listen to this next one, Mutti. You'll love it. Then I'll take you out to a café for lunch." She loped over to the record player and put on another record. The recording was older, sounding distant and even more painful. Elena brought Eva the album cover. On it was a photo of a Black man named Lead Belly. He sang with all the hope and crushing fear of the whole world in his voice.

"My girl, my girl, don't lie to me, tell me where did you sleep last night?"

"*Hier, Mutti, für dich,*" Elena said, and brought over the Nina Simone record.

"*Danke, danke, Liebchen, wie lieb von dir,*" Eva said and held her daughter's cheeks in her trembling hands and kissed her again. She wasn't so bad, this one. "*Oh, ich freue mich. Wirklich.*"

Elena took Eva out to a café around the corner from her apartment, a new place that Eva thought lovely. Eva kept the Nina Simone album on her lap the whole time, putting her napkin over it, while she carefully ate a delicious piece of chicken, with sides of rice and buttered green beans. She could tell that Elena was proud to be able to take her mother out to such a nice meal. She was so grateful, but underneath the gratitude was a resentment she tried to ignore. And she needed to ask Elena for money. Her face got hot at the thought and then, as if her daughter could read her mind, she asked, "*Mutti, brauchst du Geld?*"

They looked at each other then. It was not an easy look. It was not the first time by any means. Eva detected something ugly in her daughter's eyes. Power? Pleasure? It was not a gentle look.

"*Liebe Elena,*" she said, "I could always use some money. You know, since I stopped working . . ."

"*Kein Problem, Mutti,*" Elena said, her look softer now. "I make good tips, good money at the bar, and my rent is nothing. Here," she said, and passed her a small pile of bills. A hundred marks, Eva saw, and put them in her wallet.

"*Danke, Liebchen,*" she said, trying to smile, trying to hide her resentment.

By the time Eva emerged from the U-Bahn on her way back to her apartment, the sun had long ago stopped trying to assert itself. She didn't like walking in her neighborhood at night. The walk from the U-bahn to her building was a long one, and some of the blocks were wholly desolate, free of buildings or people but full of cement and rubble and garbage bags and syringes, with the occasional mangy, feral dog, sometimes foaming at the mouth, undoubtedly diseased and dangerous. She hurried, the record Elena gave her tight under her arm, her head ducked into her coat. She got to the block before hers, full of older three-story houses in various stages of decline. Her enormous white building loomed high above her. The same three skinheads came out of the empty hole where there once was a doorway.

"*Fräulein, stehenbleiben,*" one said to her. The other two began to laugh.

Eva started to walk faster.

"*Fräulein, Mädchen, stehenbleiben! Haben Sie mich nicht gehört? I sagte halt!*"

Eva continued to walk very quickly; then she decided to run. They were well behind her now and weren't following her, but she kept running. Then she tripped on a crack in the sidewalk and fell forward and put her arms out to catch herself. She heard the record crack. She was mad at herself now. She stood up with some effort and brushed off her coat. Her hands were shaking. She pulled the record out of the sleeve, and indeed it was badly cracked. She put it back anyway, carefully, as if she could somehow salvage it, and with her chin up, walked home.

CHAPTER 4

She had come home and taken four of her sleeping pills right away. Her hands were red and scratched from her fall but not bleeding. She poured a large wine. Her legs were throbbing. She had walked up the ten flights of stairs very quickly. She could feel them pulsing under her hands as she took her hose off, noticing a red bruise on one of her knees from her fall. But her legs didn't hurt, just throbbed. No, nothing hurt right now but her heart. She placed the Nina Simone album in the stack. Well, she'd just put on an old record, one she'd heard a million times. They still were beautiful. She put on a Paul Robeson album, and with his almost unheard-of deep bass range, he sang "Ol' Man River." She drank the wine quickly and then took out a small bottle of cheap brandy, which she usually saved for guests. The pills must be working a bit, she thought, because a warm calm came over her. The little bottle felt heavy in her hand; she carefully put it down on the table and began wiping the dust off of it with a napkin. Where was her Hansi? She could call him. She could hang up if Paula answered. She had done that once, years and years

ago, and he asked her about it. She couldn't lie, not to him.
He was all she had, really. He told her if she called him again,
he'd never see her again. But that was at the beginning of this
all. That was maybe nine years ago! She could try. She could.
She drank the brandy and sang with the record, "Take me to
the promised land."

When the record stopped, she played it again and poured
herself more brandy. Why not call him? What did she have to
lose? Maybe he was never going to come see her again anyway.
She hated when she got to thinking this way. It was no good.
He loved her as much as she loved him. They were lovers. They
were. She tried to explain it once to Liezel. What it meant to be
lovers. Liezel listened quietly on the phone, but Eva knew she
didn't understand. Not that it was easy to explain. It wasn't like
marriage. It wasn't like her marriage to Hugo or Liezel's marriage to Fred. It was a constant waiting, not a constant in your
life. It was intoxicating, painful, brutal. Well, marriage could
be brutal too, but for the opposite reasons. For the mundane-
ness of it all. Not for the fleetingness, for the scarcity. Being a
lover was like being in constant hope. It was like having faith.
Or belief. She was better suited to be a lover than a wife. She
was best at faith. Better at faith than at living, she felt, a third
brandy in her hand.

She walked out to the phone and dialed his number, which
she knew by heart, although she hadn't called him again, not
since that once. But she knew his number, just in case. What
if there was some emergency? This wasn't an emergency,

she knew; it just felt like it was. She knew Elena's number, too. But she wasn't going to call her. She was too ashamed. Elena would tell her to move, to leave her tiny apartment, her neighborhood that had turned wild. She wouldn't have any empathy.

She dialed, but hung up even before it started ringing. When she returned, she got into bed, leaving the record skipping. She tossed her underwear on the floor and put both hands between her legs. Hansi. Closing her eyes, she put two fingers inside herself and with the other hand she rubbed and rubbed, trying to climax, but she was too drunk, too out of it, too drugged.

She woke very late the next day with a terrible headache, the record still skipping. Before peeing, she took the needle off the album, examined the record quickly—it was fine—and turned off the player, and ran to pee. Then she looked at the clock—one o'clock. At least half the day was gone. That was some accomplishment.

Had she tried to call Hansi? How shameful. She rose awkwardly and sat at the edge of her bed. The moon had shone so brightly through her window, and she had sung herself to sleep. She thought of the broken black vinyl. And then, of how high she'd been afterward, drinking brandy after taking pills. She couldn't come, but she had made peace, though. She had fallen asleep giddy and singing and smiling to herself. God loved the world. God would take care of her. Those had been her final thoughts. Now the dark thick blackness descended on her; now she hated God. Hated Him for not protecting her. She tried shaking her head, but the black thoughts settled in her. She lay on her stomach, panting, hands in her crotch, and this time, hungover, yes, but sober and wet and swollen, aroused, she made herself come quickly.

There was a little wine left in the bottle, and she poured it into a glass and drank it down in one gulp. She took a night pill to take the edge off her hangover. She sat on her bed and took off her smelly hose. If Hugo were alive, he'd never have let this happen to her. If Hansi'd been with her, they wouldn't have done this. People were afraid of Hansi—even the skinheads, she'd noticed. For a moment, she wished Paula dead. It was a thought that poured into her mind, from who knows where, like black, cold, thick water. She wished her dead, dead, dead. She needed him. She needed her dead.

A knock on her door. "Eva?"

Krista. She got up, put her hose under the bed, and opened the door.

"*Hallo, Krista,*" she said, trying to compose herself.

Krista asked, "*Geht's dir gut?*"

"*Ja, ja, komm rein,*" Eva said. She hated this about herself. When her emotions took over. She wasn't in the mood to share her weakness right now. Something about wishing Paula dead was still in her. She had never wished anyone dead.

Why her? Why not the skinheads? It was as if that dark liquid thought was now something else, its own thing, spreading in her blood.

"Du wirkst ein bisschen verstimmt," Krista said.

"It's nothing," Eva answered coldly. "There was a long line at the wine store when I was there. I didn't want to miss you, so I came back and didn't get any wine." Eva gave a short laugh. "I love my wine."

"Klar," Krista said, *"weiß ich doch, dass du Wein liebst,"* and she laughed. *"Vielleicht kann ich ja nochmal für dich zu dem Geschäft gehen, wenn wir den Brief geschrieben haben?"*

Eva relaxed. Krista, her helper. She didn't really have the money for another bottle; her budget was very tight. But she needed it. But now she had money from Elena. *"Das wäre wunderbar,"* Eva said. She took out her stationery and an envelope, then retrieved the stamps she had bought on the way to Elena's, and the two women sat at the table.

"I'd like to try to dictate in English, but sometimes, I know I won't have the words," Eva said.

"It's okay. I can translate for you," Krista said, her hair still unwashed, her purple sparkling sweater gray under the armpits.

"Can I get you a coffee?" asked Eva. She didn't want to make coffee, but she should offer the girl something.

"Nein danke," Krista said. "I had one right before coming over, with my mother."

"Okay," Eva said. "Let's begin." She dictated, Krista wrote, and then Eva gave her money to get her wine.

"I'll put this in the mailbox for you, too," said Krista, "and bring you your wine."

"*Das ist so lieb von dir,*" Eva said and without thinking, hugged the girl. Today seemed to be a day that her thoughts were not her own, or that someone was thinking for her. Soon it would be over.

CHAPTER 5

Dear Maggie,

I was so happy to get your letter. I think it's wonderful that you want to come back to Berlin. And congratulations on finishing university. You must be proud of yourself, and your mother must be proud of you too. I saw Elena, and I know she is not very reliable about writing letters or calling, but I can say that she would be very happy to have you stay with her. Of course, I wish you could stay with me, but you know I don't have much room here. We can visit frequently—more easily than when you were here last! Now that the Wall is down. I hope you'd like to. There will be no 24-hour rule for you returning through Friedrichstrasse, but this I'm sure you are aware of.

Things have changed much since the Wall came down. I am happy to see Elena without much trouble and there were always things I liked about the West— some hand lotions, and so on—but my neighborhood has become quite awful. It was never this way before. There is crime now and it makes me very sad. Sad for the world, and sometimes scared. Also, there is garbage and litter on the streets, and in my neighborhood, this too is particularly bad. The buildings, which the GDR didn't take the best care of, are now often left to crumble and burn. Of course, new things are being built all the time. I shouldn't complain. But it is a lot of change, some good, some bad. Many people have left, but not everyone. Krista and her mother are still here next to me. Do you remember them? Krista remembers you and looks forward to seeing you.

Have you heard of the singer Nina Simone? If I could ask one favor of you, it would be to bring me a record of hers. Of course, I most likely could find it here now, too. But I know she is American—but she also, like me, hated America, the racism, the capitalism, and moved to Paris, did you know?—so maybe it is very easy and inexpensive to buy her records there. I lost a record of hers, and badly miss it. It had the song "I Loves You, Porgy" on it. I think it is the most beautiful song I've ever heard.

Please call on the hall phone. Here is the number— 001 49 3 453 7769. I so look forward to seeing you. I am sure you could make a good life here. Or just a good year. I have the most confidence in you. And I am happy you are in love. I didn't forget that! And I look forward to meeting your man, too.

Viele Busserl,
Tante Eva

CHAPTER 6

December came. Krista knocked, calling, "Eva! A letter!" Drying her hands from washing clothes in the sink, Eva let her in.

"*Komm, setz dich,*" she said to her.

Krista asked, "*Darf ich dir vorlesen?* It's from Maggie."

"Yes, please do. I'm going to finish washing. Then I'll sit with you."

Eva went to her wardrobe and opened the small drawer and took out the letter opener. Krista read:

> *Dear Tante Eva,*
>
> *I was so happy to get your letter! I got it only two weeks after you sent it. Can you believe it? It used to take months. And sometimes, my mother told me, you never got her letters at all.*
>
> *I am living at home in the suburbs with Mom and Dad and working as a waitress at a restaurant called Friendly's. It's not a lot of fun and it shouldn't be called Friendly's. The customers are often not friendly and the tips are not that great. But it's a job, and I'm trying not to*

spend any of my money so that I can soon come to Berlin! Living at home is helping me save—I don't have to pay rent—and also, my parents are feeding me, which helps me save, too. But I hate the suburbs. I can't wait to be in a city, a real city. Not that Chicago isn't a real city, but it's not Europe.

I think I'll have enough money by January. So, that is when I am planning on coming. I will write Elena again. I haven't heard from her and so I worry that it won't be okay for me to stay. But if you say it is, I will believe you. Also, it's possible Thomas will come with me as I mentioned, I think, in my earlier letter. Anyway, thank you so much for welcoming me, and for talking to Elena.

Thomas is living in Chicago with some of his friends. I get to see him pretty regularly, though. He is older than me, did I tell you that? It made me think of you and Hugo. He's not that much older than me—Hugo was 30 years older than you, no?—but he's in his thirties and he's so intelligent and such a fighter. He cares about the same things we do—justice for the poor, the end of hunger. You will like him, I think—I hope!

I'm sorry to hear about the crime in your neighborhood. Take care of yourself! I can't imagine crime in East Berlin—although I guess it's not East Berlin anymore, is it? Wow—I just can't wait to see it all. And I will bring you Nina Simone records! And have you heard of Billie Holiday? You would love her, too. I will bring her records, too. They are much cheaper here than in Berlin, I think. Do you have a CD player? I think not, so I will bring records.

I'll call you as it comes closer to January. Take care, Tante Eva.

Deine,
Maggie

CHAPTER 7

Maggie was right. There was a time when she didn't even get Liezel's letters. Yes, it was true, there were many things wrong with the GDR. But there were good things, too, and the whole world seemed to be overlooking them for the bad.

There was no crime. No one was hungry. It was true that the food had not been as high quality as in the West, but everyone, *everyone*, had food. Everyone. This meant so much to Eva. And to Hugo—Hugo who knew what it meant to suffer, who knew what hunger meant.

And everyone had an education. No one was denied that. Everyone had a place to live. Of course there was corruption—people high up in the Party had nicer homes and cars. The elite, of which Hugo was a part, had quite good lives. But no one suffered! No one suffered as in the West. Of course there had been corruption in the West, too, and still was, but now it was all coming east. Slavery, child labor, poverty, illness—these were all things from the West. Crime! The skinheads. In the GDR, they'd have been thrown in jail. Fascism was illegal. Always on the same corner. Always looking for trouble. In the GDR, they'd be working. Everyone had a job. That was another thing—no unemployment. None. Jobs for everyone. That was why there was no crime—because everyone had to contribute to society. Everyone was given the opportunity to contribute to society in a positive way. In many ways, there was endless opportunity. All this talk about no opportunity was just silliness. They didn't have the luxury goods of the West, but who needs those? Who truly needs that stuff?

When Maggie had been visiting in 1986, Eva had taken her out to dinner at the Fernsehturm, the revolving restaurant at the top of the tower in downtown East Berlin. It had been dark, around eight o'clock. Maggie wore a nice skirt and blouse, and Eva, of course, was in one of the few dresses she had, with her hair poofed and sprayed. She didn't go to the Fernsehturm often. It rose out of the dark streets, an outrageously tall, white abomination of a building. Its nickname was the Asparagus. Eva had been there only a few times, and not for years. It was a special occasion. As they walked down the street, Maggie looked left and right. She looked up and down the street and at the buildings. There were no shops. No lights. Eva knew that this was on her mind. Eva knew how different West Berlin was—not to mention Vienna, Paris, and New York. But what made East Berlin particularly stark—and she knew this as well—was that one could see over the Wall to the West if one were high enough, which they were about to be, to see the blinking and shining of its wasteful lights. It was the contrast that was so harsh. Eva had long ago made peace with that.

She'd made peace with all that when she'd moved to Berlin with Hugo. With Hugo, she never questioned anything. He made her believe. He made her know what was right, what was good and just. Although he hadn't been with her in a very long time, that belief never left her, that the East was better—that they could live a more moral life there, and that that was what truly mattered.

In the restaurant, one could really see for miles. Eva was proud of this and wanted Maggie to be impressed. But Maggie mostly seemed bewildered. There were many long tables, and they were seated at the end of one of them, across from each other. The restaurant smelled of heavily spiced meat, rich and warm, a bit gamy. Soon people were seated right next to them, complete strangers, elbow to elbow at the same table. In the West, this was not how restaurants were. It was the knowledge of that that made Eva's face burn. Maggie was polite, but Eva knew she found the experience strange and not to her liking.

Well, it was all gone. All those things peculiar to the East: the waiting in lines, the darkness, the eating at communal tables. Gone, gone, gone. What would Hugo think of all this now? The end of the GDR? She was glad he wasn't around for it. Death often has a purpose, she thought. It's not only cruel.

CHAPTER 8

Hansi was there. Suddenly, out of the blue, without any warning. She was coming down from her apartment to run some errands and there he was. Not yet noon, a cold day, the middle of December. She was dressed very warmly—her thick wool coat, a hat and scarf, gloves and boots. But she had carefully put on her makeup, as she did every morning. Hans! Her Hansi! Standing to the right of the doorway, where it was darkest. A fur hat and his fur-lined leather coat.

They embraced. He kissed her, held her face in her hands and kissed her, his lips warm and wet and covering her mouth. The taste of stale tobacco and mint.

"Come up! I was just going to the store. I can go later. Come up! You look so cold. It's warm in my apartment."

"*Nein, nicht sofort. Erst möchte ich etwas mit dir anschauen.*"

He took her around the corner, and there sat a shiny car, an American car.

"*Was ist das? Was ist los, Hansi? Woher hast du dieses amerikanische Auto? Wo ist dein anderes Auto?*"

He laughed, showing his big, healthy teeth. They were

brown from cigarettes and coffee, but strong and thick. "Don't you like it, Schatzi?" he asked, running his bare hand along the trunk. It was goldish yellow in color. Eva peered inside. The seats were also yellow, and made of leather.

Oh, to have her Hans call her Schatzi. Hugo never called her that—Hugo didn't believe in terms of endearment. He thought they were belittling. They disagreed with his ideas of rightness. But Hansi wasn't like that. He was her Hansi, and she was his Schatzi.

"Well, it is beautiful." Eva said, timidly. Then she laughed. It was always something with her Hansi, always something new and strange. He was a mystery—she loved that about him. But she couldn't help to ask how he was able to buy such a car. He had always had privileges, she knew, but this car was another level of decadence. "*Sehr schön. Sehr sehr schön!* How is it you can afford such a thing?"

Hans looked at her sharply. She had made a mistake. "That is none of your business, silly woman." Although he smiled a fake smile, his eyes were mean, and he pinched her cheek too hard.

"*Aua!*" Eva said, and held her hand over her cheek. Without looking at him, she quietly apologized. "*Entshuligung, Hansi.*"

"*Geh,*" he said. "Let's go for a ride!"

They drove and drove, through the crowded streets of Berlin, Hans proudly showing off his car, classical music from the radio playing loudly. It was too loud for talking, the music, but that was okay with Eva. Hans wasn't much of a talker. They often didn't talk much. No, it was enough to be next to him. That was all she wanted, truly. To be next to him. In the car, in bed. But she didn't much care for the music. She knew this made her seem uncultured. That, perhaps, it even made her a bad German, or a bad Austrian, that she didn't care for Beethoven, or Mozart, or any of them, really. But with her Hansi next to her, even the music didn't bother her.

"Shall we go out to the countryside? Drive on the Autobahn? Heh, Schatzi? *Was würde dir gefallen?*"

"*I will nur bei dir sein,*" she said. It was true. Tears were in her eyes. She didn't care what they did. She just wanted to be by his side. And she wanted to ask him, where have you been for all these months? She wanted to ask him, how can you stand to be away from me for this long? She wanted to tell him that it robbed her of years of her life, when he didn't show up for months and months like that.

"*Okay, meine Schatzi.* I'll take you home."

Eva's heart began pounding. "*Willst du mit mir hochkommen?*"

"*Ja, Liebchen. Ja.*"

He made love to her fiercely. It had been so long since she'd had him, it felt like he broke her for the first time. She was bruised and sore, lying beside him. Her mouth was swollen and her teeth throbbed. She went to her sink and ran the water until it was hot and then wet a small towel so she could clean him off. She wiped his penis, his thighs. Then she rinsed it off again and wiped his neck and chest. He had grown fatter since she'd seen him, or so it seemed. It didn't bother her—nothing about him could bother her—but she noticed it, noticed that he had been gone so long that he could change significantly. And yet all that mattered was that he still loved her. And to think she had doubted it! It was always like that, when her heart was filled with doubt, he showed up. She could never doubt him for long. No. He always came before she gave up all hope—she had never gotten totally hopeless. Despair, yes, that she had felt. Without any hope? No.

"*Magst du einen Brandy?*"

"*Gerne.*"

Eva went to her cupboard and took out the brandy. It was almost all gone. There was just enough for one small glass for Hans. She poured it out and then poured herself a *Mineralwasser*.

"*Nimmst du selber keinen?*"

"*Nein, besser nicht,*" she said.

He lay there, naked and ripe and warm. Eva had put on her bathrobe—she wished it were a nicer one, a newer one.

Hans stood abruptly. "*Ach, was ist das. Scheiße!*" He walked to her cupboard and took out the empty bottle. "*Ach, Eva, I need to buy you some good brandy. This is *Scheiße*. *Wirklich!* Are you stupid? Trying to poison me?"

"*Bitte, nicht!* I'm sorry. It's all I have. You've been gone for so long." She hadn't wanted to say it. To say anything whiny or needy. Hans didn't like that.

"I'm getting dressed. We are going to get you some decent brandy," he said, pouring the rest of his glass in the sink. "Get dressed, " he snapped and threw her dress at her.

Later that night, after he left, Eva opened the large bottle of brandy, carefully pulling off the paper, which she folded and saved in drawer. It was fine brandy, from France. She poured some in a glass and watered it down with *Mineralwasser*. She looked in the small mirror in the bathroom. There was a small bruise on her cheek, and it was still tender. She touched it, fascinated. She had makeup that would cover it easily. She had just taken a shower and wore a new satin robe that he bought her at a department store. It had cost nearly forty marks. It was dark blue and shone like a jewel, with a white collar, and it was lined with terrycloth for extra warmth. It was the most beautiful thing she'd ever seen and the most beautiful thing she owned. It smelled new, not unlike the clean scent of Hansi's new car. She stroked the silky fabric, stroked her own arms. He was gone, but now he was with her, too. The brandy, the robe. And other things, too. Some good cheese and sausages. Two bottles of good German red wine. He bought them for her, but also for himself. He would be coming around, even if he didn't say so. Warm and buzzing from the brandy, she lay down in her bed and felt her sore parts with both her hands, and she rubbed her swollen self until she came, hard.

· · ·

That night, sleeping in her robe, she dreamed of Hugo. She had fallen asleep, thinking of Hansi inside of her, on top of her, loud and possessive and sure of himself. So why would she dream of Hugo? She dreamed of Hugo sitting at the kitchen table in their old house, already very old, perhaps already with lung cancer. His glasses pinching red spots on the sides of his nose, his thick gray hair standing up in tufts on his head from where he'd run his fingers through it again and again. He was looking through contact sheets in the dream, as he so often did in real life. Everything in the dream was like a normal day from their past, except where was she? She was there watching him, but she couldn't see herself. Hugo looked up from the table and took off his glasses and closed his eyes and rubbed his temples. When he opened his eyes, they were red and glowing, like a wolf's. He said, "*Meine Augen tun weh*. Can you see them bleeding? They are shedding tears of blood."

But they weren't shedding tears, not tears of blood. They were red and glowing painfully at her—full of terror, full of bodily anguish. And then in the dream, his eyes turned into Hansi's eyes, and the redness was that of the devil himself, and Eva was alarmed in the dream and started to back out of the house. She couldn't see herself doing it, but she could feel her body moving, backing up. "*Nein, nein,*" she said, but now she was awake, her head pushing into the pillow.

CHAPTER 9

She was not happy with her dream. How could she have such a dream, after her Hansi came back to her? Was it guilt? Hugo was not even alive, and she still felt guilty sleeping with another man. A man she'd been sleeping with for ten years. Hugo was her husband before God, and she was sinning. Could that be the message of the dream? Yet they had not been faithful to each other even in marriage. The dream felt like a supernatural punishment, and now awake, she was mad that she was so afraid after such a nice night with her lover. Why couldn't God let her have her happiness?

She had been raised Catholic. Sometimes, even after marrying a Jew and living an atheist life in a godless country, she still felt more Catholic than anything else. But it was her kind of Catholicism. Angels and devils communed around her, and occasionally, late at night she heard them. They were God's creatures, all of them, the spirits and the living, as was every living breathing organism on the planet Earth.

Hugo would tease her, when they were first married.

Tease her about her prayers and her rosary and her talk of the saints. Saint Jude. Saint Michael. Saint Anthony. She had loved these saints as if they were her brothers growing up in Austria—her keepers. Indeed, she prayed to them to return their father from the war—he had been a prisoner of war for a year, in France—and her father was returned. When her stepmother kicked her out of the house—her house, with her sister and brother still in it, the house she had run so well since her mother's illness, since her mother's death—she had prayed to them again, to give her a man, to find her a husband. And they had; they gave her Hugo. So although she knew that Hugo was the man she should marry, and although she knew she should live her life in a Communist country, where all people were equal, where no man ruled over another, she did not find it easy to give up her God, her Christ, nor her saints.

Hugo would say, "When we die, we rot in the ground and our physical body returns to the earth, the earth from where we came. The liquid inside of us is salt water, our tears, our urine. Do you know why? Because once, we lived in the ocean. And now we carry it inside of us. No God created us, as we are now, walking the earth. We climbed out of the ocean, like other beasts, and evolved into what we are now, slowly, over millions and millions of years."

And perhaps it was all true. That they came from the ocean. But God may have overseen the whole process. And millions of years to us may be a second of time to Him. And while Eva had seen pictures of the flesh that rots in the earth, she knew a spirit life existed, too. What else could it be, this consciousness that was uniquely hers, but a spirit? A spirit that would someday meet with a greater spirit, with that from where she came, from where they all came?

And perhaps Hugo, the man who believed in nothing but molecules, perhaps Hugo's spirit was trying to tell her something. That he was some sort of Devil now—but no, then it was Hansi's eyes. That he was still more interested in his photographs than anything else? That he was suffering in purgatory? That he needed her to help him be set free? That his spirit was intertwined with Hansi now?

He hadn't been the best husband. And she wasn't a great wife much of the time. But they had done their best. Well, much of the time they had done their best. It was chic and liberal to have lovers in their circle of friends—the writers, painters, poets, and other photographers. It had been easy for Eva, too. She was very young and perhaps she wanted something that Hugo couldn't give her. Hugo was older than her father. It had been a tacit agreement. Sometimes, thinking back, Eva wondered if he had encouraged her to take lovers. Even insisted, in some way. And he, too, had other women. She didn't mind him sleeping with them, but one or two of them would end up spending too much time around their house. Particularly the last one, the one right before he died. Behaving like his personal, youthful nursemaid. Eva had disliked this very much. True, she was busy taking care of their daughter, but not *that* busy. She took good care of him, too, fed him, kept the house neat, looked after things, the mending, the errands. And when his health started failing, her nursing skills were very helpful. She took good care of him through it all. She didn't like that girl in her house, fussing over him, no, but that she shared his bed hadn't bothered her so much.

She had one lover from the hospital. Another nurse, not a doctor. He was even younger than she at the time. Karl. Hans reminded her of Karl—not in appearance. No. But in temperament. He had been her cruelest lover, this young man, a boy really, maybe twenty-three years old, not that she was much older than he, but she was married and a mother. Her husband was dying. Karl would have her over to his flat. She remembered when he broke it off with her. He was very drunk. He smelled of vomit. She had come by his flat after work, a bit desperate. She knew it was ending. He had taken her from behind, in her asshole, and she'd bled and cried. Then he told her to leave. To not come back. *"Kuh,"* he had said. *"Du bist eine dumme Kuh."* She was shocked—her body hurt, and her head felt numb from it all. She went through the next few days in a haze, quiet and subdued. But she hadn't been surprised by his behavior, by the names he called her. She knew she had behaved desperately. Perhaps it was the only way he thought he could get rid of her. It did work. She never bothered him again.

Her Hansi had a temper. He could get angry.

There had been other lovers, too. At some point, there had been many fights with Hugo. Not that he ever yelled or called her names or was anything but gentle with her. No, he was too good for that. Too good for her, she had often thought. But his gentleness wasn't always separate from a kind of passivity. Often she wondered if he felt anything for her. Once she had been drunk and he had a lover and she knew it and it was maybe his first and so she had been hurt. Angry. She remembered, with much shame, yelling at him. *"Warum bin ich nicht genug? Ey? Was stimmt nicht mit mir? Passt dir meine Muschi nicht? Eh? Warum sagst du nichts? Wie kannst du so ruhig bleiben?"* And he never said a word; he just let her go on like that. Until she threw a lamp at him. They never replaced that lamp, either. A lamp in the GDR wasn't the easiest thing to come by. And she'd foolishly broken one. The side table remained without one thereafter, a reminder of her outrageous behavior.

It hadn't been all bad, but one always remembered the bad times more vividly. Pain is memorable, and the daily goodness of life is not. Eva knew that. No, it hadn't been all bad at all. So why such a nightmare? Maybe she'd go to church. That was one good thing about the Wall being down: she could easily go to real churches, not like the ones that had been in East Berlin. She didn't go to church often, and she rarely went to the same one more than twice. She wasn't looking for a priest or a minister. Just a building, just a space to commune with her God.

. . .

There was an Eastern Orthodox church in Kreuzberg, one she'd passed by on her visits to Elena and admired. She took the U-Bahn and got out a stop early to walk. Since Hansi's visit, her legs hadn't been bothering her. The walk made her feel good, energized her by getting her blood flowing. She had no heavy bags to carry and she wasn't just standing—that never felt good; to just stand there almost always caused aching and throbbing. She walked at a nice pace, briskly, and just a few blocks really and soon she'd be kneeling. Or sitting. She preferred to kneel. The sun was out and it wasn't warm, but it was a beautiful winter day.

Christmas was coming, a holiday they never celebrated when Hugo was alive. Since his death, she'd always done a little something on Christmas Eve, the most important night for German Christians. This Christmas, now that Hansi was back in her life and she was getting on with Elena, maybe she'd try to have a small *Tannenbaum* in her apartment. And put some candles on it. Yes, that would be so nice. Even if Hansi couldn't get out to see her that night, maybe Elena would. And if nothing else, she could have Krista and her mother, if she was up to it, over for some *Kuchen*.

Eva pushed on thick, tall doors and they swung easily inward, revealing the dark, long room of worship. It was cold inside, but it was open and empty, just how she'd hoped. So quiet, too, a demanding sort of quiet. A heavy, rich quiet. Her boots clicked loudly on the stone floor. She walked down the center aisle until she felt she'd found her spot, then she slipped into a pew. There in front of her was a red cushioned plank to kneel on. With her head bowed, she began praying: "Our Father, who art in heaven, hallowed be Thy name. Thy kingdom come, Thy will be done, on earth as it is in heaven . . ."

She prayed the prayers she knew so well and then prayed for Hans, for Maggie, for Elena, for Liezel and Fred. And for Hugo's spirit. This was always a bit difficult, as Hugo was a Jew and an atheist, but that didn't mean she couldn't pray for his soul. Lastly, she prayed for herself. "Dear Lord, My Christ and Savior, please let me be with Hansi. Please let him come visit me regularly. Please don't take my Hans away from me. I know he is married. I know this is a sin, but it is the only thing in my life that brings me joy. Please don't make it end. *Bitteschön. Bitte, bitte, bitteschön.*"

It was dark by the time she left. She wanted to stop by Elena's, even though she had forgotten to call beforehand. Well, it was her daughter; she could stop by her very own daughter's without calling first, no? In the darkness, she felt much colder, and after all that time kneeling in the cold church, it would be nice to be in Elena's warm apartment. Maybe Elena would even have a brandy for her.

The stores were still lit up and the young people busied themselves inside. Kreuzberg was so different from her neighborhood! It was a different world, a different land, really. The land of prosperity, of lovely canals, of bistros and pubs. Eva knocked, and Elena opened the door without so much as a question.

"*Du bist zuhause! Ich war in deine Gegund, und da dachte ich, ich schau mal bei dir vorbei, ich hoffe, ich komme nicht ungelegen . . .*"

"*Nein, Mutti. Du kommst nicht ungelegen.* Come in, Mutti. Come in. "

"Elena, Liebchen, you must ask at the door who it is, and not just open the door to anyone who knocks. I worry about you."

"Worry about yourself, Mutti. Kreuzberg is very safe these days. Unlike your neighborhood."

"It's so warm in here! You don't mind if I sit a minute and warm up before heading back, do you?"

"Not at all. I have been working on a painting, and I could use a cigarette break. Come, sit down. Would you like a beer?"

"Do you have a brandy? It might warm me up better."

"I'll see what I have," she said, removing herself into the kitchen.

Already Eva felt warmer. The apartment heated so nicely, unlike her own. The room was full of lamps and much brighter than Eva's apartment. In this way, Elena was like her father—always aware of lighting. She was a true artist, like her father. She was like her father in many ways, although not as mild-mannered as he was.

"*Hier, Mutti, dein Brandy.*"

"*Danke.*"

"*Bitte.*"

The brandy burned as she poured it generously into her mouth. Immediately, she felt her cheeks flush.

"I had a dream about your father."

"*Ja?*" Elena sat in front of her mother, on the floor. Her legs were crossed in a yogic position, and she had a tall pint of beer in one hand, a cigarette in the other.

"Yes. I came to pray at a church near you today. You know the church, on Carl-Herz-Ufer? I dreamed he was at our old kitchen table, looking at contact sheets. His eyes were red, like the devil's. It was a nightmare. It was awful. I fear he may be in purgatory, or worse. He was such a good man. Why wouldn't his soul be at rest?" She didn't mention that his eyes had turned into Hansi's eyes.

"Oh, Mutti. Don't worry about Vati's soul. Worry about you. All dreams are about oneself, according to Freud. So, I worry why you are having nightmares."

"I'm fine. Don't worry about me. I recently had a wonderful day with Hans. He bought me a new robe."

Elena stood up and walked to the record player. "So, *der Schweinehund* is back."

"Don't call him such names! You two were friendly once. How can you say such things?"

"Well, I think he brings you more unhappiness than happiness. Married men are no good. And he's got something
rotten about him. I'm afraid of him for you. Anyway, how
can you go to church and sleep with a married man? I don't
understand, Mutti."

"That is between God and myself, Elena." Eva finished
her drink. She shouldn't have said anything. It had been
pride. She tried to show off, to make herself feel good,
look good. Pride was Lucifer's sin, and look what it did
to him.

"He has too many secrets, also," Elena said and looked
sharply across the room at her mother. She was holding a
record in her hand, and Eva just wanted her to put it on.
"But you know that already, don't you, Mutti?"

What did she mean by that? Of course he had secrets.
Everybody had secrets. It was a bad subject, Hans, to bring
up with her daughter. "Play the record, Elena. Let's talk
about something else. Let's talk about Maggie coming. Have
you heard from her?"

"*Bis jetzt noch nicht.*" She dropped the needle on the
record. It was Lead Belly, the record she played for Eva last
time. For a moment, Eva thought about her Nina Simone
record. She saw in her mind the skinhead, the fall, her hurt
hand. It was there still, in her little pile of records. She
wouldn't say anything to Elena about it. Eva worried Elena
would blame her or, worse, start harping on her neighborhood.

My girl, my girl, don't lie to me . . .

She wasn't going to move, and she didn't want Elena bothering her about it.

"*Wollst du noch einen Brandy, Mutti?* Then you must go. I need to get back to my painting."

"*Ja, bitte, gerne noch einen. Danke, Liebchen.*"

CHAPTER 10

It had been a little more than a week since Hans's visit, but it seemed a lifetime to Eva. For the past few days, she'd just wanted to sit around her apartment—she didn't want to leave, not even for a minute, in case he stopped by. She needed some things, too. Milk for her coffee, bread and cheese. She started to eat the tinned food in her cabinet. And she tried not to drink all the brandy, either. She really hadn't had much, except for last night. Last night, in her beautiful blue robe, she drank two brandies. Big ones, maybe it was really more like three. And the moon was full and round, directly outside her window. She played a record, a gospel record. "Sweet Jesus, I am worried. Sweet Jesus, I am sore. Sweet Jesus, I don't even think that I can go on anymore." She sang along, the curtain of her window pulled aside so that she could feel the moon on her, see its light. She missed Hans.

She fell asleep at some point with her robe on, which she did before, but this time it was different. When she woke, it was very wrinkled, and damp, too, from her sweat. Now she would have to clean it. She woke tired and ashamed. Ashamed of her melancholy, tired from the late night and the brandy.

There was a knock as she made her coffee. Could it be Hansi? Maybe someone let him in. She looked terrible! She put her hands to her hair and opened the door nervously.

"*Grüß dich*," said Krista.

"*Grüß dich, Krista, komm rein,*" Eva said, disappointed and relieved. "*Ich dachteschon, du wärst mein Freund. Und ich sehet so schrecklich aus!*"

"You don't look horrible, Eva. I like your robe. It's beautiful. But I was a bit worried about you. I heard you last night. And, you know, it's two in the afternoon. Usually you are up. Even if you don't go out, we can hear you up and about by this time. I'm sorry, I was worried."

"You have nothing to be sorry for. That's kind of you to worry about me. I'm fine."

How could a young girl like Krista know what loneliness was? Or her mother, who had her daughter to comfort her?

"Would you like some coffee?" Eva asked.

"Yes, thank you."

"Milk and sugar, *richtig*?"

"*Bitte.*"

"Then maybe I could get your mail for you? Have you heard again from Maggie? Is she coming?"

"Thank you, Krista. I must go out today. I haven't been out for days. This is the last of my milk. So I'll check my mail on the way down, but thank you."

The girl looked disappointed. Maybe Eva should have just let her.

"*Aber, vielleicht kannst du mir morgen meine post hochbringen. Morgen hab ich nicht vor, rauszugehen.*"

"*Okay. Morgen dann.*"

"And maybe you can tell me where a record store is. Where they sell old records. I have lost one recently."

"I don't know, Eva. I'm sorry."

"*Macht nichts.* Elena will know. I will just ask her."

"I don't listen to old music. But I am very interested in new music. I thought I could talk with Maggie about new music. She lived in Boston and there is very good music in Boston and New York. And Washington, DC. I wonder if she likes the same music I do."

"Perhaps," Eva said. "We'll soon find out!"

Krista smiled. Eva didn't like her smile, because her eyes didn't smile with her mouth. "Yes, she's coming soon."

Eva was grateful for Krista and her visits, but she sometimes found her a bit demanding. And sour. She felt bad, too, which made her less patient. But when she felt bad, when she'd had too much to drink, she often took extra care. She washed vigorously in the shower. She teased her hair and sprayed it. She put on deodorant and cologne, then applied her makeup: powder and then mascara and eyebrow pencil, then lipstick. She had taken extra morning pills and felt so light she could barely catch her breath. She dressed very carefully and carried her robe in a brown paper bag. She would take it to a cleaner Insanely expensive, but worth it. The only problem was that she'd have to be without it for a few days. And she was scared.

Scared that the skinheads would bother her again. They hadn't bothered her in a while now. Then again, she hadn't been out for days.

Taking the stairs slowly, she thought, perhaps he'll be there! Perhaps! Just be there, hiding in the shadow of the door. Maybe if I walk slowly enough, she thought. Maybe then. Maybe if I'm patient.

When she got to the door, she opened it and stood outside. It was cold and dark. A bit of dry, hard snow fell from the sky. She didn't look frantically about. No, she looked straight ahead and waited. If he were there, he'd come to her. If he were there.

CHAPTER 11

The next morning, Krista knocked. "Eva! A letter!"

Eva was awake, drinking coffee.

"Ich komme," she said, letting the girl in.

"It's a letter from Maggie. Shall I read it for you?" Krista asked, sitting down next to Eva.

"Gerne. Danke." Eva stood to get her letter opener. And then Krista read:

Dear Tante Eva,

How are you? I am sorry I haven't called you on the hall phone. For some reason, I prefer to write you. I am not much of a phone person. I did call Elena, though, and spoke with her. I am due to arrive in two weeks! Isn't that exciting? The week after Christmas, Tom and I fly to Berlin. Elena has agreed to let us stay there and we will pay her rent. This is temporary, until we find our own place. I really want to find a place near you, in the old East Berlin. I hear there are some wonderful, exciting neighborhoods now in the East. How is your neighborhood? Elena says it's not safe and that she tries to convince you to move. Can that be true? I have read that the crime rate has gone up a bit. I am sure it is temporary. I am sure that when things straighten out— when Berlin gets used to being unified again, or rather, when all of Germany gets used to being unified, that Berlin's crime rate will drop again.

I can't wait for you to meet Tom. He is a Communist, but not a Stalinist. Maybe you would think of him as a Socialist. He has spent time in Cuba and loves it there. He is the type of man who would have been fighting against Franco in Spain. I am so in love, Tante Eva. I think we will get married and have children.

I've saved up tons of money from my job. I was so good! There were days when I wanted to shop—buy clothes, makeup, go out to eat. But I really learned how to control those materialistic thoughts. Americans are such consumers. But Tom and I together should have enough to last us until we find work. I know we don't have work visas or anything, but Elena thinks we could get some cash work in a bar, and Tom has some ideas, too. I also heard it's not hard to find work teaching English and that you can get a visa issued once you have a job pretty easily. And that some institutes pay cash. We'll see. It'll be an adventure, but I also have faith that we can make it work out. With Tom by my side, I feel I can take on the world. I am bringing you some records, too. The Nina Simone you asked for and some others.

I will call you from Elena's—there is no need to meet me at the airport. We will talk and talk, just like we did when I was there in, what was it, '86? I can't wait!

Viele Busserl,

Maggie

CHAPTER 12

Hugo appeared to her in her sleep again, over her, while she lay in her bed, somewhat cold in her slip, her hands wrapped around her fleshy arms to keep warm, to stay protected, and in a gesture of missing her blue robe. Her robe was safely in her wardrobe, but she no longer wore it to sleep. Picking it up from the cleaners and taking it back to her apartment had caused her such stress. She was so afraid the skinheads would take it from her. The cleaner was far away, and they gave it to her wrapped in plastic on a hanger. It shone through the plastic, glimmery and new. It was awful. She didn't take it, because they didn't have a bag for her to put it in. She returned the next day and put it carefully in a large brown bag. Even that had made her worried. Worried that someone would notice the large brown bag. So then she rolled the robe around the hanger, the plastic protecting it, then put it in the bag and rolled the bag up, too, so it wasn't so large, so conspicuous.

All that trouble to hide it, and then all the fear. Then it was the one evening the skinheads weren't there, lurking in the doors and at the corner. It was a bitter-cold evening. Perhaps they were drinking in a bar, keeping warm. They'd be back, cold or not. She knew that.

The whole ordeal had upset her greatly. Her heart was a pounding mess, and her hands shook so badly she could barely hang up the robe by the time she got up to her apartment. She took extra sleeping pills and let herself have one brandy that night. No more brandies, she thought. Not until he comes back. And no more wearing the robe to sleep. Only while awake. It killed her to take it off at night; she felt lonely without it. But she couldn't put herself through that again. She could try washing it in cold water, in her sink. But that seemed risky, too.

And instead of Hans, Hugo appeared to her. Hugo, his eyes back to normal, sad, brown, mournful eyes. In the dream, Eva woke up in her bed and saw him over her. Then she noticed he was inside of her, too. Making love to her the way he used to, slowly, deliberately, his eyes on her face the whole time. With Hugo, it was almost as if she had no body, only a face.

She was shocked he was there, making love to her. She said, *"Hugo, was ist los? Was tust du? Du bist tot!"*

"Ja, Liebchen, ich bin tot. Aber wir sind in der Welt der Seelen. Du hattest recht. Ich war blöd, ich lag falsch. Es gibt ein Leben nach dem Exitus. Ich dachte, du wärst blöd, dämlich. Ich war doof, nicht du. Ich."

"Aber warum bist du hier?"

"Du bist meine Frau, oder?"

"Ich habe einen Freund, Hugo. Es tut mir leid."

"Ich weiß, Eva. Ich weiß alles. Eines Tages wirst du das auch."

He got off of her and walked to her wardrobe and opened it. Inside shone her new robe. She turned her face in shame. When she looked back, Hugo had turned into her father. He was wearing her robe.

"Hure," he said angrily, and began walking toward her.

It was then that she woke.

CHAPTER 13

Her father had been a harsh man. They all knew he loved them. But Franz Stiller was not a gentle person, and when he was angry with his children, which was frequently—they were too loud, they were not clean enough, they left a mess everywhere, they didn't bring in any money—he hit them.

Her brother had it the worst early on, when their mother was still alive and their father was still around, unhappy with his work as a tailor in Leoben. No one paid him enough, he had to work too long of a day, his hands were sore, cracked, sometimes bleeding.

Then when the stepmother came, Liezel had it the worst. Eva was just thrown out, she didn't have to stay and endure the wrath of Maria. Liezel did. Broken noses, even a broken arm once. Maria took over. Franz, older, less volatile, let her do everything. Including beat the children.

But when their mother was alive, it was their father who terrorized them. He terrorized them one minute, and the next minute, drunk on shnapps, he picked them up and put them on his lap, singing *"Eine kleine mausi,"* crawling his fingers up their arms and making them laugh. They laughed nervously, worrying that his mood would change. Sometimes it did change, quickly, like a sudden storm. But usually by the time he was drinking schnapps and lifting them up on his knee, he wasn't going to get angry again. No, it was done by then, the rage and punishment.

Hugo was not that kind of a father. He was the opposite. He never even raised his voice with Elena. He would say to Eva, who ended up having to do the discipline, "Don't crush her spirit, woman. She is only a child. Let the world crush her spirit later. You don't need to do it. Let her be."

And Eva agreed often, but not always. Elena needed some guidance. Someone had to potty train her, for instance. If it were up to Hugo, she would have shat in her diaper until she was ten. Really. He just didn't care.

It was strange for Eva to be the disciplinarian. It wasn't fun. She tried not to hit and yell, but did on occasion. Mostly, she indulged her only daughter. But she hadn't been perfect. Unlike Hugo. Hugo had been perfect. In his mind, he was without fault. And in Elena's mind, too. Her father had been perfect. Eva couldn't help but agree with the both of them herself. Hugo was perfect. She was not. She was given to tempers, she was a bit moody. She was weak.

The final fight between Maria and Eva was a long time coming. She'd been criticizing Eva since the day she moved in. The way she did the dishes, set the table, her cooking, everything. Maria took over cooking on day two after moving in. It was that swift. Even if Eva followed the grocery list perfectly, Maria would harp at her over her shopping.

"The celery is soft! Did you pay half price for it? You better have paid half." Then she'd count Eva's change. Give her a stare. She'd been in control of the money from day one.

Finally, Eva, as mild-tempered as she was, lost it. She was mopping the kitchen floor—something she used to do once a week, but Maria had her doing it every day—and Maria came in.

"You're just moving the dirty water around the floor! That's not cleaning!" she yelled. Eva stopped and stared. For a moment she felt what she often felt. She felt sorry for Maria. Eva's father didn't love her. Maria was ugly—fat, the face of a man, hairy chin, unruly curls on her head the color and coarseness of straw, long breasts that fell to her waist. Of course she was mean. Eva threw the mop at her stepmother and ran, ran three blocks to her best friend Saskia's apartment. The next day, in the middle of the night, with Willie's help, she collected her few belongings. With Saskia's mother's help, within a week, she found a job in Vienna and moved.

Eva, seventeen, worked as a live-in maid for a wealthy family, a family that had gotten rich during the war. They were dreadful people, but Eva was very lucky to get the job. She had left with only half the clothes she owned. Her suitcase contained two very well-made dirndls, made by her own mother and herself, a wool nightshirt, and two pairs of stockings and two pairs of underwear. She felt greatly indebted to Saskia's mother for getting her the job. For months, she sent her a portion of her paycheck. It hadn't been the agreement, but it seemed the right thing to do.

Eva had been hired quickly. Her good looks, her nice manner, her healthy, big-boned body—these were all good qualities for a maid. She cleaned windows and hauled large bags of food and waxed the floors.

There was another girl who lived in the servants' quarters and was their governess. She was from Poland—Liliana. It had been Liliana who introduced her to Hugo. Hugo lived in a residency run by the Russians for the dispossessed, the poor, the homeless. More than half of the people had been in the camps. Hugo had been in Buchenwald. A Jew, and a Communist. It was a miracle he was alive.

She knew immediately that he would be her husband. He had kind eyes, the slowest, most gentle touch. His intelligence was tactile and quiet; he was unlike anyone she'd ever met. She took care of him—he had suffered from malnutrition, overwork. He had a lung infection, and he'd lost a toe. But he had a camera. He bought one the minute he could. He was from Vienna—his entire family was dead. His apartment no longer his.

"Come with me to Berlin. The Party is strong there. We will be taken care of. The Russians freed me. They saved us. Who knows that Fascism won't spring up again here, in Vienna? There are criminals everywhere. The family you work for? I'm sure they made their money off the backs of dead Jews."

It chilled Eva to think that, but it didn't surprise her. What did that make her, then, working for them? Liliana would soon go back to Poland. She was saving her money. Eva, too, had been saving, but to go where? She didn't know. Now she knew. Now that Hugo was with her.

They were married in a civil ceremony. It was almost two years after she'd been chased out of the house in Leoben. It was the first time she wrote home to her father, to tell him she was married, to tell him where she lived. And to Liezel, whom she missed so much, her baby sister. She must have grown so much. Eva had one picture of her, and it wasn't even current when she left. It was a school picture of Liezel at age five, two braids on the sides of her face, smiling.

It would be almost a decade before she saw her sister again. After their father's death. Before Hugo's.

CHAPTER 14

Eva was coming out of the stairwell on her way to get coffee and soap when he stepped in front of her. Hansi! They embraced and kissed hard on the mouth.

"*Komm, Schatzi, wir gehen zu mir nachhause. Paula ist mit den Kindern in Polen. Nur du und ich, eh? Wunderbar, oder? Ich kann dich ganze zwei Tage haben!*"

"*Oh, Hansi! Ja, wunderbar, wie schön. Lass mich nur kurz ein paar Kleider holen, und Toilettensachen . . .*"

"Okay, okay, hurry up, though."

"Won't you come up and stay warm while I fetch my stuff?"

"No. Hurry. I'll wait here." He moved from foot to foot and lit a cigarette.

"Okay. I'll hurry."

It was not the Cadillac in which they'd driven around last time, but his old car. Eva didn't say anything, because she didn't want to make him angry.

"I need to make one stop. It's on the way, don't worry," he said, and he grinned at her, grabbing her thigh. She was beside herself with anticipation. She could barely keep herself from grabbing him back, pulling him on top of her right there, in the car.

The roads became quiet, the houses few and far between. They couldn't be far now. Indeed, it seemed they had passed Wandlitz, the suburb where Hans lived. Hugo had been very critical of Wandlitz, and Eva understood, but it seemed hypocritical, too, that Hugo, as a Party member and part of the elite intelligentsia, had lived differently, too. Of this, Eva became very certain, after his death. After she and her daughter were told to move.

But it was true, Wandlitz was even quite a step up from where Hugo and she had lived. Everyone who lived there worked for the government. They all knew one another, but they had privacy. It was a small neighborhood of beautiful three- and four-bedroom houses, all privately situated, secluded in the gorgeous, ancient woods. The war had destroyed everything, but not the trees of Wandlitz. There was a private restaurant just for the inhabitants of Wandlitz, and a private grocery store that imported goods from the West.

As they drove, Eva realized they weren't going there, to his home in Wandlitz. They must be going to his cabin. But what did she really know? The cabin was small, with a wood-burning stove. A three-room cabin, on a lake in Güstrow. No one for miles. He had taken her there, years ago now, and during warmer weather. It was almost Christmas! How cold would it be there?

Hans pulled into a gas station, the first building of any kind they'd seen for an hour. "Wait here. I won't be long."

It was dark—the building, the gas pumps—no lights anywhere. Could someone possibly be here? Eva felt uncomfortable. She watched the shadow that was Hans disappear behind the low building. Maybe there were apartments in the back? She waited.

Twenty minutes passed. Where was he? He wouldn't leave her here, abandon her. But she was cold. With the motor off, the car wasn't heated. Anger welled up inside of her.

It was never about her. She was just there for the ride. She knew this. He wanted company, but she wasn't the reason why they were out here, no.

Another twenty minutes passed, and Eva, against all reason, decided to get out. She needed to move her feet! She needed to move her body, the cold was settling in and she felt sick with it. She got out and left the door of the car slightly ajar. She didn't want to get locked out if, God forbid, something had happened to Hansi.

She followed the way he had gone, toward the building and around to the right and then behind it. There, at the back of the building, was a window, some room not visible from the front, and a light on inside of it. The curtains were drawn, but she could hear men yelling. Eva was scared, but even more scared to return to the car alone. The yelling stopped for a minute. She thought she heard a toilet flush and then the door opened and there was Hans, red-faced, carrying a huge box. A man sat in the back of a dingy room, smoking. He smiled at Eva.

"*Mein Gott, was machst du hier? Raus!*" Hans yelled at her and then threw the box at her. "And take this. Take this to the car."

The box was enormously heavy; she was afraid she would drop it. Soon Hansi was behind her, with another box.

"Get in the car."

Now what? She sat in the cold car, but she was upset enough not to even worry about being cold. Hans went back to the building, then back to the trunk of the car with another box, and then one more. Then, finally, he got in next to her and they drove off in silence. When they arrived at the cabin, Hansi turned to her and slapped her. "Stupid woman," he said. "Never follow me when I'm doing business. You'll get yourself in trouble."

Eva put her hand to her face. Hansi removed her hand and put his hand on her cheek. His big mitt of a hand was like an ice bag on her hot, stinging face.

"*Ich liebe dich, eh,*" he said. "I don't want you getting hurt, *verstehst du?*"

It was the closest thing she'd get to an apology from him. And he knew better than her. Still. She didn't like getting slapped.

"*Ich weiss, ich weiss,*" Eva said.

Hansi built an enormous fire in the wood stove. The cabin was so small, it heated up quickly and Eva felt the romantic nature of the place. The remoteness, how it was just the two of them for miles. He put two large eiderdowns on her and brought her a brandy. When he got in bed next to her, everything was forgotten. Everything was perfect.

CHAPTER 15

It was Christmas Eve, Eva's favorite night—favorite moment
of all the year. Elena was having her over. It would be just the
two of them. Her brother had invited them to Austria, but neither wanted to spend the money. Some year they would go.
But she was too prideful to ask for him to pay for her tickets,
and he never offered to, of course. Eva had asked her daughter to come to her house, but she said, *"Warum, Mutti? Deine
Zimmer sind so trostlos. Lass uns Weihnachten bei mir feiern."*

"But you must get a tree and wrap a present. It can't be just
us drinking beer with no . . . I don't know . . . with no atmosphere."

"Don't worry. I'll get a tree."

"I can bring candles. And other decorations."

"Toll. And bring some brandy. I'll have food, too. Not just
beer. I promise."

The only disappointment was that Eva couldn't wear her robe.
Hans had bought her a new dress during his last visit, which
she wore, but it didn't make her feel quite as special as her robe

did. It was a tight red dress with big, puffy sleeves. She felt a bit
garish in it, but she knew, too, that it was a nice dress. It wasn't
that she wasn't grateful; she just, if she had a choice, would
always be wearing her blue robe. Maybe she could find a blue
dress somewhere.

Berlin was beautiful during Christmas. The entire city was
lit up, music poured from people's houses, from the shops. Red
bows and silver icicle decorations hung everywhere, even from
the humblest apartment buildings. *"Fröhliche Weihnachten"* was
heard from every corner, from nearly every person, even those
who normally were sour. Eva could feel Christ's spirit. Feel
God's spirit. She drank a very strong coffee mixed with brandy
before heading out to the U-Bahn to go to Elena's. Her cheeks
flushed and she put the two gifts she had for her daughter in a
bag. One gift she left behind, the one for Hans. A shirt that she
agonized over—was it too bright? He liked bright colors. It was
orange, a rusty orange. She imagined him in it, imagined him
kissing her full on the mouth, saying *"Danke, Schatzi. Dank-
eschön."* She left the shirt behind, carefully wrapped in shiny
gold paper. She left it on her neatly made bed. In another bag,
she had a bottle of brandy and a big sausage. And in another
still, her Christmas ornaments—the heavy candleholders, the
silver glass balls, the gold angel that rested on top of the tree
instead of a star. She knew it was a bit different, but she loved
it. She had used it all her married life, all her adult life. And
in the ornament bag were new boxes of candles. It all felt a bit
heavy, but she was full of life. It was the day Christ was born!

Her savior! She knew it wasn't as important as Easter, but it was her favorite holiday. It was.

Kreuzberg was alive and full of joy. Everyone—the punk rock kids, the hipster families, the artists and even the Turks, who didn't believe in Christ—everyone was friendly and smiling.

Elena, too, was joyful.

"Hallo, Mutti! Fröhliche Weinachten, liebe Mutti!"

"Oh, fröhliche Weinachten, meine Tochter, meine Elena!"

Her apartment looked so nice. Eva was touched that her daughter had done this. There was a nice white tablecloth, one Eva had given her, on the table. Some new chairs were placed around the table. They were used, Eva could see, but her daughter had done this for her, found some chairs so she didn't have to sit on pillows on the floor. And a tree! A *Tannenbaum*! It wasn't as small and scraggly as she'd expected. Not that she thought badly of Elena; it was just that trees were expensive and hard to haul about. But the tree was beautiful—full, green, fragrant of pine. Tears came to Eva's eyes. God was good, God was love. There were a handful of ornaments already on the tree. Including a beer can turned upside down. Well, Elena always had a sense of humor. And a very funny idea of art.

"I brought brandy, *mein Liebchen. Hier! Für dich. Für uns!*"

"Danke, Mutti."

"Und eine Wurst!"

"Danke, danke! Warte, Mutti. Lass uns darauf mit Brandy anstoßen."

She sat near the tree, the room aglow with lamps. Elena brought her a drink and she began unpacking the goods carefully. Her fingers moved with ease, despite her excitement. She carefully placed the two gifts under the tree and then began putting on the ornaments. She attached the candle holders to the branches, carefully placing a new candle in each one. There were the silver balls, the glittery red balls, the gold ones, too. She could hear Elena singing in the kitchen as she prepared food for the two of them: *"Stille Nacht, Heilige Nacht, Alles schläft, einsam wacht, Nur das traute, hochheilige Paar, Holder Knabe in lockigem Haar, Schlaf in himmlischer Ruh! Schlaf in himmlischer Ruh!"*

Eva stood and joined her daughter, walking into the kitchen, abandoning the tree for a moment, singing: *"Stille Nacht, heilige Nacht, Hirten erst kundgemacht, Durch der Engel Halleluja, Tönt es laut von fern und nah, Christ, der Retter, ist da! Christ, der Retter, ist da!"*

Later, full and drunk, they opened presents. She had bought Elena a set of warm wool gloves and hat, and three expensive pads of drawing paper. Elena had given her a lovely, bright purple silk scarf, which she put on immediately, and a book on a photographer, an artist named Nan Goldin. The book unsettled her, but she knew her daughter meant well, that she was trying to share her interests with her mother. Hugo never attempted to share his love of the arts with her; he was content to have it be a separate thing, his work, his photography. But Elena wanted her mother to understand her interests.

And Eva tried, sometime more than other times, to understand what moved her daughter.

"*Komm, Mutti, lass uns Fotos von Vati angucken,*" Elena said and took out one of the books of Hugo's photographs that she owned. They sat flush against each other. The candles were lit; they had lit them at midnight, singing "*Stille Nacht*" one more time. Soon they would have to put them out. It wasn't safe.

Elena had all of Hugo's work. Eva had a few random photos, here and there, mostly of her daughter. Maybe one or two of Hugo and of herself. But Elena had books and books of Hugo's work. She was the legal manager of his estate and the sole beneficiary. Eva had been named estate manager and beneficiary when Hugo died, but as soon as Elena was old enough, she gave the responsibility to her daughter. Elena was a better person for the job. There were the occasional requests to reprint his work, and even requests to include a photo in a show. Elena had organized a beautiful retrospective of his work five years ago, too. That was the last time Eva had really looked at his pictures. And even then, she didn't look much—she glanced more than looked.

She knew he was a good photographer, but she didn't care so much. So often, his picture taking seemed a way of not dealing with the world. Hiding behind the camera, trying to capture his subjects, and giving nothing of himself. Photography wasn't a brave art. Perhaps no art was brave. Perhaps it was always a way of hiding oneself and stealing from others.

The book Elena had out was mostly family photos. Carefully printed, black-and-white pictures on thick paper. First came photos of Eva and Elena. Eva with her daughter, who was five at the time, in the backyard of their house. Eva's hair, still thick and blonde, her skin smooth. Gravity had not called yet. Was she twenty-three in those pictures? Something like that. Wearing a dirndl she remembered well, a green, flowered bodice, a lavender apron. Her breasts were high and round, showing at the top of her dress. In the pictures, Elena could barely sit still. She had been a child! Eva knew she'd been a child, but to think of it too much was painful. Then came more photos of Elena: Elena in the kitchen, her head cocked sideways, a piece of fruit in her hand. A painfully huge grin. Elena quiet, a rare thing for her—she'd been such an active girl—sitting on her bed, naked, right after a bath.

And there were many photos of Eva. One photo was of her face, up so close that she looked strange, as if she were staring at her pores in the mirror. Eva hated that picture of herself. And Eva naked in bed, right after he'd made love to her. Eva in the kitchen, cooking. Eva in the backyard, reading. There were photos of Christa Wolf, the writer, a friend of Hugo's. And of Fred Wander, another writer. Strange, how Hugo mostly socialized with writers. Strange how young they all were. It almost seemed impossible.

And then the photos jumped to years later.

Eva asked, *"Was machen diese Fotos in diesem Album? Sie sind von viel später."*

"I know. But they are of Liezel. And I put them in, because she is family. And with Maggie coming, I thought it would be nice to have them."

Liezel, during the one and only visit she made to Berlin. Right before she moved to Paris, where she then met Fred. Her dark hair, shiny and healthy, framing her face. Her eyes—she was all eyes. Slightly turned up on the sides—cat's eyes. She had grown to be even more beautiful than Eva. Her baby sister. And then more photos of her, many without her clothes. Liezel in the guest room, naked, looking straight at the camera, but shyly covering her childish breasts. Liezel in the yard, sunning topless. Liezel, sitting up, most likely on top of him, her face covered by her hair, her body contorted with passion.

Well, it was the sixties, the beginning of them at least. That was what Eva thought, if she had the misfortune of thinking about that time. Both she and Hugo had lovers. Why did her sister feel like such a betrayal then? Her sister. Her baby sister. She didn't know where to direct the anger, toward Hugo or Liezel. She was furious that they made her hate them, because she did hate them. For a very long time. But not forever—how could she hate them forever? Hugo died; Liezel moved so far away. Everything changed. Other things became important.

But looking at these photos on Christmas Eve, the blackness came over her. She wished it away. She prayed without saying a word. God, make it stop. The hate. She closed her

eyes. When she opened them, she looked at Elena. Elena—
her eyes hard. Eva hated her. An image of herself bashing her
daughter's head into the table came over her. She was outside
of herself now, looking down on herself and Elena. She exhaled
hard—she had been holding her breath. Mother and daughter held each other's gaze. Then Eva grabbed Elena's skinny
forearm and pushed it down on the table, holding it there. She
wanted to kill her, but at least she would maybe bruise her.
Despite Elena's youth, Eva knew she could physically domi-
nate her. She knew she was bigger, and crazier. She had that
blackness, the thing that hardens the heart cells.

"Au, Mutti, du tust mir weh!" Elena said, trying to pull her
arm away from her mother's grasp.

"Warum heute Abend?" Eva asked, leaning into her daughter, her grip strong. Elena's hard eyes changed—she was afraid.
Good. Eva then stood and went to the bathroom and peed. She
had one pang of guilt, then she brushed it off.

"Ich hasse diese Fotos. Wirklich. Abscheulich," Eva said when
she returned and then she went into the kitchen to pour one
more brandy. When she came back, Elena had put the photos
away, but she was smiling strangely. Her fear was gone. It
was as if she thought she had won some battle, surmised Eva.
Well, Eva thought, let her see how she feels when she's my
age. She hated Elena now for her youth. She often hated the
young. The hate would pass, she knew. Just as the blackness
would drain out of her.

"That must have been very hard." Elena said. "Vati wasn't

the angel I always thought he was. I know that, Mutti. I still love him, the memory of him. But I know he wasn't perfect."

"Good heavens! It's Christmas Eve. Talk of joy and love, Elena. Your father was an angel. Perfect, no, but an angel, yes. Angels were just as human as us once."

"Mutti, stay here tonight. Yes? It's too late for you to go back to your place. Stay here with me."

"*Danke, Elena. Okay, Ich bleibe. Danke.*"

CHAPTER 16

She remembered so vividly the day Liezel arrived for that visit, as if her mind contained color photographs of that special day, a catalogue of pictures imprinted on her brain. Her baby, her baby sister, whose cuts she kissed, whose tears she wiped, whose breakfast, lunch, and dinner she prepared. Who was so afraid after their mother died. So needy. That day, as she waited at the train station, was one of the happiest days of her life. She remembered the dress she wore—blue cotton, with little white flowers. She remembered the smell of her cologne, 4711, a citrus floral, and the smell of her own nervous sweat. Liezel, the baby she wished was hers, then later became hers. Sometimes she thought, I willed my mother to die. I wanted Liezel all to myself, and God answered me. God gave me what I wished for.

"*Jetzt, bin ich deine Mutti, Liesele.*"

"*Du bist nicht meine Mutter,*" she had answered, angrily. "*Du bist meine Schwester. Du bist meine Eva.*"

"*Ja, aber jetzt, wo Mutti bei den Engeln ist, will ich deine Mutti sein.*"

They slept in the same bed. Liezel's warm body and her hot breath warming Eva on many a cold night. Liezel had needed her but didn't realize that Eva had needed *her*.

To leave Liezel with Maria, who hated their father's children from his dead wife, seemed the cruelest thing in the world. But what was she supposed to do? What could she have done differently? Honestly! She couldn't have taken Liezel with her—no one would have hired her. She'd had no choice.

Now she was coming to visit, on a vacation from her job as an au pair in Paris. She had written her and explained how well she was—how she got a position with a wealthy family in Paris. How she spoke French and Italian, from spending time as a maid at a hotel in Italy.

Liezel had stayed a child in Eva's mind. So to meet the beautiful adolescent—the young woman, really; although she was seventeen, she, like Eva at that age, was undoubtedly a young woman—was shocking. Eva had been well into her her marriage, and tired of it, and her daughter was growing independent, busy with school and friends. Hugo and she were sleeping with other people.

She wanted to ask Liezel about Vati and Willi, but she didn't. She wanted to hold her sister in her arms for hours, but she didn't. She couldn't stop touching her, though. At one point, Liezel moved discreetly away from her touch. It was too much touching, Eva knew.

Did she sleep with Hugo out of revenge? Revenge for abandoning her in Leoben? Liezel must have thought that Eva didn't care, but that wasn't true. They never talked about it. To this day, they'd never talked about it—about Liezel's feelings of pain and fear when Eva left, nor about her sleeping with Hugo that summer. Why talk about it? It wouldn't change things. It wouldn't change a thing.

But how could she ever forget? The shrieks of ecstasy, no different from shrieks of pain, coming from the guest room, her sister's shrieks, her husband causing them. She would take Elena on long walks. She visited her friends, their friends really, as Eva had no friends of her own. No, everyone was friends with Hugo; their life together revolved around him, his status as a photographer, an artist of importance in East Germany. Eva was just the wife, a simple nurse, perceived as a simple woman, she knew. She didn't have artistic ambitions or inclinations. She knew what people thought of her. Perhaps she wasn't creative, but she wasn't naive, either.

Wolf and Greta Biermann were their neighbors as well as their close friends, and they had a daughter Elena's age. Wolf, the poet, later left Berlin altogether. His work was often the work of criticism. This, to Eva, was not very exciting work. It was often very clinical, almost dogmatic. She preferred emotional art. Of course, political art could be emotional in its own way, but it wasn't personal enough for Eva. Not that anyone cared about her opinions.

She treated Greta like a friend. Greta was a painter. Greta was an artist. She said to Greta, "Hugo is sleeping with my sister."

"Nein, das kann nicht sein, Eva."

But it *was* true. Eva didn't push it. She'd just had to say it, even if only to one person, even if that person didn't believe her. And, of course, later, she realized that Greta was sleeping with Hugo, too.

CHAPTER 17

Christmas Day was always somewhat of a disappointment after the joyous light of Christmas Eve. She had slept in her daughter's bed, warm and loved, and today she headed back to her apartment with her gifts—the odd, disturbing book of photographs, the lovely scarf. After she dropped them off, she decided, she would go to Mass. A good Catholic Mass, perhaps in one of the beautiful neighborhoods, perhaps in Charlottenburg. She had asked Elena if she wanted to go, but she had declined.

"I'll see you in a about a week, Mutti. Come here the day Maggie and Tom are due to arrive. We'll have a small party for my cousin."

"*Wunderbar, Elena. Danke für alles.*"

"*Danke dir. Du bist so lieb. Meine Mutti, meine einzige Mutti.*"

"But of course I'm your *only* mother! You're so silly, Elena."

"Take care of yourself, Mutti."

Eva resented the tone. "Don't worry about me. I am more than fine. I'll see you soon. *Tschüsschen!*"

• • •

No one was on the U-Bahn. That was the first thing that made her melancholy. And then, the weather had turned so dark and cold. A horrible wind blew. It wasn't yet eleven in the morning and it felt like night.

The skinheads were out on their corner. In this weather, on this important day. Hatless, their leather coats seeming brittle and useless in the cold, they passed a bottle. Clutching the bag that held her scarf and book, she thought briefly of crossing the street. It was Christmas day, it was only eleven in the morning.

Then, there hiding behind the men, was Krista.

"Krista, bist du das?"

The girl stumbled forward, her head uncovered, her face raw with the cold and alcohol. *"Hallo, Eva. Hier, das sind der Kurt, der Peter und der Johann."*

"Aber . . . komm mit mir, bitte. Komm—ich bring dich hoch in eure Wohnung. Your mother is worried about you, I'm sure."

Johann, the leader, passed Krista the bottle. She swigged it, and breathed out hotly afterward. "My mother thinks I'm at the soup kitchen today. That's where I spend every Christmas. Every Sunday." They all laughed. "That's what my mother thinks." They laughed so hard, Krista nearly falling over.

"Krista, darling."

"Our little Krista is celebrating Christ's birthday with us," said Johann. He pulled her, and she stumbled toward him.

"Yeah, Eva. *Fröhliche Weihnachten,*" Krista said and grabbed the bottle again.

"*Genug*, you greedy girl," Johann said and pushed her away.

Eva, with regret, began to walk away, leaving Krista with those abominations. "Eva!" shouted Krista. Eva turned and looked at her. The poor girl. It broke her heart. "Don't say anything to my mother, please? My friends here wouldn't like that."

Eva turned around and resumed walking, as fast as she could, but not so fast that she couldn't help but hear Krista say, drunkenly, "She's an old cow, that woman. A nasty, dumb cow."

When she got upstairs, wheezing with the effort, a small brown package sat leaning against the door. It was a miracle no one had stolen it. Where had it come from? There was no mail on Christmas. Eva put her bag down and picked up the package. It was from Maggie. It had been opened. But it was here, for her, intact. Strange that it had been opened; those things didn't happen anymore. It used to be that all of her mail was opened; that was just how things were. But now? It must have been someone in the building. Maybe she could find out by asking the postal worker for their building. Maybe he would know. Her heart sank. It probably had been Krista.

She poured herself a brandy. Yes, it was early, but it was Christmas. She wasn't going to make it to an early Mass, but she would make it to an evening one. Inside was a Nina Simone record: *I Put a Spell on You: Nina Simone in Concert*. And a letter from her niece. She read it alone, without Krista helping her. She never really needed Krista's help, but she wanted to be kind to the girl. Krista calling her a dumb cow. She was drunk. She was trying to impress the skinheads. Eva contemplated telling her mother. Even though Krista was drunk, Eva still was hurt. Krista was good to her. But still, maybe Eva should make some distance from her.

She read the letter.

Dear Tante Eva,

I know I am going to see you soon and you asked me to bring you a record, but I thought I'd try and send you one for Christmas. Fröhliche Weihnachten! Nina Simone records are not as easy to come by as I thought, although her CDs are very easy to buy. I think I may have to get you a CD player. Of course, you may be like my dad, who dislikes the CD very much. He claims they sound inferior to the vinyl record. He still only listens to records! Anyway, we can talk about that all very soon!

Mit viel Liebe,
Maggie

Christmas Day. What a gift. The day itself, her daughter's kindness the night before. She could put Krista out of her mind. She could pray for Krista. Say Our Fathers and Hail Marys.

She put on the record. She listened to Nina Simone sing to her man that she loved, begging him not to let some other man take her, handle her, drive her mad.

Oh, the suffering of others. Krista was suffering too. Suffering was the birthright of all of mankind, but perhaps more for some.

CHAPTER 18

The day came for Maggie to arrive. Elena had gone to the airport, to surprise Maggie and Tom. Eva sat in Elena's apartment,
nervously waiting. It had been so long. She'd been a young
teenager, in the real sense of the word, when she was here last.
And even though she'd taken herself all over Berlin, studied at
the Goethe Institute, done all of those things alone here, she
was still being taken care of by her parents, by her parents'
money. Which wasn't a bad thing. Maybe Eva was a bit jealous
of her privilege. She knew Liezel herself envied her daughter's
privilege; this was ironic, as Liezel was the one providing the
economic support, the coddling, the middle-class life, the trips
abroad—everything. She wanted to give her children everything she hadn't had as a child, but then she resented them for
not appreciating it. Silly! Children don't appreciate their parents, no matter what. And how could they know how fortunate
they were, having known nothing but privilege? They had no
reference, no framework, really.

Maggie did try to understand. With her political activism,
her work with the mentally ill—a college job she was very

proud of—her aspirations to make the world a better place for the poor. Her profound criticism of the United States. Of course, here is where the irony ran deep. Not only did she loathe her mother for all things capitalist that she saw her as standing for—personal advancement, exploitation, materialism—but her ability to be so critical and harsh seemed to stem from the very education that Liezel was so proud of giving her daughter.

The truth was, Eva didn't really care much for politics. She cared for the human race, and she had moral ideas both vague and specific, but politics? She had trusted the chancellor. She had trusted Hugo. She hated to think of the poor and uneducated, the malnourished and homeless. But she would never vote, would never go to a rally. Indeed, she avoided all such things. Politics embarrassed her, but morality made sense. It seemed the minute people adopted a strong stance, they became hypocrites. It just seemed unavoidable. Better to be humble and trust in God, trust in what was good and right, on a daily basis.

She could hear them on the stairs, the loud American voices, one distinctively Maggie's and one from a man, speaking English, the laughing. Elena's voice, too, seemed loud, in her accented but good English. Eva stood nervously and smoothed her skirt, touched her hair, put a finger to her lipstick. Her spoken English was not great, but they were here to improve their German, she reasoned, to practice their German.

In they came, carrying heavy backpacks, and Elena, too, helping with a duffel bag. Maggie still looked young, but she was not exactly the same. How could she be? Is that what Eva wanted, for Maggie to still be a wide-eyed girl, in thrall of everything new to her in the world? In jeans still, as Eva imagined her, but with a tight-fitting black sweater, and larger breasts, a black coat draped on her arm. She carried herself differently; she stood more upright, more securely. Her hair had changed, too—it was bleached white-blonde and cut fairly short. She had grown up, as Eva supposed she would. But she still seemed like a girl. She still was, perhaps. What it takes to grow up, college, even a lover, can't necessarily deliver. Her skin had dark spots on the chin, and as Eva came closer, she noticed they were acne. They hugged excitedly and kissed on the cheeks, and then Maggie broke away and said, "Tante Eva, this is Tom, Tom Bellen. My boyfriend."

"How do you do," Eva said and shook his hand.

"Nice to meet you," Tom said.

But something was not right with him. His hand was clammy, cold and moist. He looked very pale and thin. Perhaps it's the jet lag, thought Eva.

"The flight must have been difficult. You both must be tired and hungry." She and Elena had made some sandwiches beforehand.

"It wasn't so bad," said Maggie. "I guess we are tired. But we ate on the plane. We even requested vegetarian meals, so that was nice."

"We made sandwiches, but they're not vegetarian," Eva said. "I didn't know. Or I forgot."

"Well, I'm not really a vegetarian, but Tom is," Maggie said, somewhat embarrassed.

"Sit down! Sit down! Would you like a beer then?" Elena said. It was fairly early in the day, but Elena drank beer all day long.

"That would be great!" Tom said, lowering himself to one of the pillows. He was very lanky, all legs and arms. He sported a ponytail, which Eva thought quite charming. One didn't see them so often anymore. Certainly in Kreuzberg, but she never imagined them on American men, just aging German hippies.

"I want to thank you, Maggie, for the Nina Simone record you sent me. It was such a treat."

"You're very welcome, Tante Eva."

"Nina Simone record," Elena said. "I gave you a Nina Simone record, Mutti."

"I know, I know, Elena. Maggie gave me a different one. A live recording." She maybe shouldn't have said anything. She still didn't want to tell Elena about breaking it. She still had it, in the hopes of getting it fixed. Silly, she knew.

Elena went into the kitchen and returned with beers. "*Prost!*" they all said, and clinked glasses.

Tom looked straight at Eva with his watery, tired eyes. She adjusted her skirt, touched her hair. "Maggie has told me so much about you, Eva," Tom said. "About your life in Berlin, in East Berlin. About your husband, Hugo." He added, "And you, too, Elena."

"*Von mir wohl eher nicht, eh?*" Elena said dryly.

"I'm sorry?" Tom said, confused, looking from one person to the next. His face was long and narrow, like the pictures Eva had seen of Frank, Maggie's father. The veins in his forehead were green and visible. He seemed too thin, much too thin. But maybe that's what vegetarians look like, she thought. She remembered during the end of the war, when meat was almost impossible to come by.

"Tom doesn't speak German very well," Maggie said. "*Aber ich möchte mein Deutsch verbessern. Hoffenlich klappt das.*"

"*Aso, machts nichts,*" said Eva. How would they all stand each other? Already, Elena was being cheeky. "Tom, where are you from in America?"

"I'm from Connecticut. From Darien, Connecticut. But I haven't lived there in years. I lived in New York for four years, then Boston. Now Chicago. And now Berlin, I guess." He grinned and raised his glass before drinking some more.

"Tom doesn't really talk to his family anymore," Maggie explained, somewhat proudly. "They are very conservative people. Republicans."

Tom nodded. Eva wasn't surprised, but still found this information a bit disturbing. Regardless of how different our parents are from us, we should still remain in some contact. She thought of how much pain her own estrangement had caused her. Well, they were young, Tom and Maggie. In a few

years, who knew how they would change. And it was natural
for children to rebel. Elena hadn't always loved her, Eva knew.

"How was your Christmas, then?"

"Tom and I don't really celebrate Christmas," Maggie said.
"In America, it just seems a terrible excuse to shop. Well, I
shouldn't say we don't celebrate it. I worked in a soup kitchen
that day."

Eva had a flash of Krista with the skinheads.

"And I was with my family for some of the day. I guess
what I mean is, Tom and I didn't buy lots of useless gifts for
everyone. You know, partake in the materialist gluttony. That
we didn't do."

"*Aber deine Eltern haben dir doch bestimmt etwas zu Weihnachten geschenkt,* no?" Elena asked.

"Yes," Maggie answered in English. "They gave us money
to give us a start here in Berlin."

"*Wie erfreulich für dich!*" Elena said and then finished her
beer.

"I know," said Maggie. "I'm grateful. I'm grateful to be
here."

She has changed, thought Eva. Five years ago, she would
have been shy and reddened when Elena teased her. Now she
stood firm.

Elena and Eva ate the sandwiches quietly, from plates on
their laps. They all drank another beer and then looked at
Elena's studio, at her long, funny sculptures, partly figurative,
partly vegetal. Tom, in particular, was impressed. And then

Elena showed them their room. They looked greedily at the bed. The four of them stood in the doorway.

"You must be tired," said Elena. "I will leave you to get settled and have a nap. *Ja?*"

"Later this week, you must come to my apartment for some coffee," added Eva, as she took her leave. "Or we could meet at a café."

"I want to see your neighborhood. We'd love to come for a coffee to your apartment. I have so many memories from visiting you five years ago. I want to see it. I'm sure it's changed so much, the neighborhood, that is."

"It has changed."

"Berlin just feels different, just from coming to the airport to here. The Wall being down . . ."

"Yes, it is a time of change. But I trust our leaders."

"Ah, Mutti, this talk of trusting politicians! Enough!" Elena said.

Maggie and Tom looked at each other.

"We've heard good things about Kohl," said Maggie.

"I'm with you, Elena. All politician are crooks," said Tom.

Eva reached for her daughter's arm. "Let's go, Elena. *Schlaft gut!* We'll see you soon then." She didn't want to talk of politics now. She hugged her niece again and put on her coat. Elena walked out with her mother.

"Let's have one more beer, Mutti. To celebrate."

Eva could feel the beers already. But it was a special day, the day Maggie arrived. At this point, she was not going to do anything else with her day, not run errands, not clean her room. "Okay. *Warum nichts?* One more beer, at a nice tavern."

Elena teased her. "Okay, Mutti, lover of nice things. You pick the tavern."

They walked along the *Ufer* of the canal. The sun was not out, but the sky held some light. Often, this time of year, it could be so dark all day long. With her daughter next to her, Eva felt a certain lightness inside as well. Perhaps it was Elena's step—a loping gait, her hands always stuffed deep in her pockets, her head bobbing with her long strides. Eva picked a tavern with very clean windows and crisp tablecloths and food announced on a chalkboard. Inside, it was all dark wood and warmth.

Elena ordered a mug of beer with a brandy on the side, and Eva had some soup and a glass of wine.

"I don't know what I think of Tom, eh, Mutti?"

"Elena, give him a chance. He just got here. He has jet lag." Her daughter, who loved her father more than anything, now seemed to hate all men.

"Yeah, but his skin is so pale. Like he's sick."

"Sometimes, airplanes make people sick. Give it some time," Eva said.

"They're only staying until they find their own place. My guess is, Maggie will find a place and a job quickly. She has that energy, the energy of someone who accomplishes a lot. Like Liezel had, I suppose," Elena said.

Eva sat quietly after that comment. The soup had warmed

her. It was true, Maggie was like her mother. A determined person. But she loved Eva, Maggie did. Eva knew this, that her niece loved her in ways that her own daughter didn't. Sometimes distance made things less complicated. A niece can love an aunt without the same baggage that a daughter loves her mother.

Their table was next to a window onto the street, and she looked out at the people walking by. So many people out on this day, probably because the sun was out. It was a beautiful day, truly. Perhaps this is God's way of blessing Maggie's arrival, thought Eva. Yes, it seemed to be a sign.

The check came and was enormous. Eva was hoping to pay for the whole thing, but she had to ask Elena for money. Elena would make extra money this month, she reasoned, with Tom and Maggie paying her for the room. Still, it embarrassed her.

"It doesn't matter, Mutti. It's no problem," Elena said, counting out the marks for the bill. "I know how small your pension is. I feel like taking the U-Bahn back with you, okay?"

"Okay, Elena, but you don't need to. I'm fine. It's the middle of the day. It's not dangerous, you know."

"I know. I just feel like riding with you back to your place. What else am I to do? I want to leave Maggie and Tom time to settle, to sleep in peace."

"You can go back and work in your studio. They won't bother you."

"I don't like to work with people around. It's no problem. I'm not worried about it. Today is special. They just arrived.

Soon, they'll be running all over the city, getting jobs, getting an apartment. I'll have time alone in the apartment, I'm sure. But I'm not in a hurry to get back there right now."

When they got to the station, Eva got out her U-Bahn card, but before she could finish swiping it, Elena had jumped the turnstile. Eva looked around; her face reddened. No one had noticed, but still . . . Elena had run ahead, and it took a minute for Eva to find her on the platform.

"What was that? Is it because the tavern was so expensive? Really, Elena, you don't want to get caught. It would be such an embarrassment. I don't need you to ride me home anyway."

"Ah, Mutti, it's just *spass*. Calm down!" She had a look of mischief on her face. Eva could smell the brandy on her. She's drunk, thought Eva.

The train pulled in, large and silent. They sat next to each other. Then Elena started singing a Tyrolean song, an Austrian song. "*Sei gesegnet ohne Ende, Heimaterde, wunderhold! Freundlich schmücken dein Gelände . . .*"

"*Elena, Stopp. Setz dich! Bitte.*" She hadn't done this sort of thing in a while—make a scene.

But it wasn't the most unusual thing for Elena to do. She cultivated her eccentricity . But she didn't embarrass Eva like this often anymore. The few people on the train looked up and then, annoyed, looked down at their papers and books again.

She stood now, singing even louder. Out of her coat she pulled a beer mug. Eva hadn't noticed her taking it. Anger dropped on her, the blackness. Now she could never go back there, to that tavern. Elena began walking along the length of the car, pulling a leg behind her, as if it were hurt holding the mug out as if asking for change, and singing, ". . . *Tannengrün und Ährengold, Deutsche Arbeit, ernst und ehrlich.*"

After a few minutes, Elena sat down next to her mother.

"Why do you need to embarrass me like that? Why?"

"Because it's so easy, Mutti. And it's fun. You need to relax."

"Well, don't get out of the train with me. Okay? I don't think it's fun, or funny. Stealing a mug. Now we can't go back there."

"We couldn't go back there anyway, Mutti, because it's *ein Beschiss*! And at least I got a mug out of it. It's nice, eh?" She held it up. "Look! I even got some change, too!"

Inside the mug were a few marks. Elena began laughing as she took the coins out.

"This is my stop. Goodbye, Elena."

"*Tschüss, Mutti!*"

CHAPTER 19

In her apartment, Eva took off her clothes and took a warm shower, then changed into her blue robe. She rubbed a heavy cream on her face—it felt dry. She was very tired, so she took two of her morning pills and made some coffee. It had been an exhausting day. Maggie was here, and so grown-up in many ways. Her figure, her confidence. And a lover with her. And Elena was acting like a child. But that was just for Eva's benefit. She wasn't going to worry about that. Elena would be a good hostess to her niece. What did Eva know? They were the young people. When Maggie had been here last time, Elena and she had gone out to taverns and clubs together, looked at art together. They had enjoyed each other, and Eva wanted to think they would again.

She put on the Nina Simone record that Maggie had given her, and listened to a song about a man in a plain gold ring. The ring showed the world that the man belonged to someone else, not to her, not to the singer.

When Maggie had been in Berlin before, after they had gone out to dinner one night in East Berlin, they walked through

Marx-Engels-Platz. It had been dark, the whole square. Now it was well lit, like everywhere, as it had always been in the West. All that energy, all that electricity, to light up the night. For what? In the East, they didn't need lights to feel safe; it just was safe. Yet Maggie had seemed scared by the darkness. Eva had been embarrassed. She knew. They all knew, all *Ostberliners*, how different it was from the West. How it was more stark, less colorful. But Eva knew even more so—she traveled to the West freely. A large group of soldiers marched by in the dark, loudly stomping their boots, and startled Maggie. "What's that? What's going on?"

"They're just Russian soldiers," said Eva.

"What are they doing here? Is there some problem?"

"Oh, no. There's no problem. They're just here. They are here to help keep the peace. They do a good job. You know, we have no crime here. I am never afraid here, like you are in the West, of walking around at night."

"I'm afraid of them," said Maggie. "The soldiers."

Eva fingered the package she had for Hans. He still had not come. And she would be lying to herself if she didn't think that he might have something nice for her. Mostly, she wanted to see him.

The package had been sitting out on her table. She carefully put it in her wardrobe. Then she took out the book Elena had given her for Christmas. Her daughter and her strange ideas about art. The pictures were ugly. Hugo wouldn't have approved. Hugo had taken gorgeous pictures. All of Goldin's pictures were in color—often with vivid, almost fluorescent shades of green and orange. Hugo shot only in black and white. Many of her pictures were of men dressed as women. Why would Elena give her such a book? Was she trying to tell Eva something? That she was gay, perhaps? Everyone was suffering in these pictures. Everyone. Suffering in their decadent lifestyle, suffering from their excess and freedom. Eva read a bit from the beginning. "My work is closest to the snapshot," wrote Goldin. Well, thought Eva, Hugo's photographs were the opposite of that. She flipped through the book some more. It wasn't that they weren't arresting, these pictures. They often were. But they never seemed anything but sad and often garish. Perhaps Elena was trying to defy her father, even though he was dead. Rebel against him, against what he stood for. Eva shut the book.

The pictures made her think of Tom. Elena was right—he did seem overly pale. And what was he doing with her niece? He was significantly older, not that she had any right to be bothered by this, considering her Hugo. She shouldn't judge him so quickly. He had just arrived. First impressions were often strong, though.

His vegetarianism Eva found quite interesting. She had heard of this from Elena, about people not eating meat because of the pain and suffering it caused the animals. Because it was morally wrong.

When the Wall came down, she was able to buy meats that

she could never get in the East. Pork, beef, chicken, duck, goose. It wasn't that there wasn't meat in the East, but it was hard to come by and then it was often very bad quality. Sometimes, after waiting a week to wait in line to get meat, she'd cook it to the find it inedible. When she started seeing Hans, he would take her to restaurants that weren't open to the general public. There they would eat goulash or steaks. Tender, good meats. It was a treat. Mostly, it seemed, she lived off of bread and hard cheese. She had never thought about the animals, only about herself. About her desire for the meat.

She read that in Cuba, every family was given one chicken a month. Before Castro, she wondered how often the families of Cuba ate chicken. Never? Elena would say, "Mutti, before Castro, things were better in Cuba." But Eva didn't think Elena was right. Was Tom a more moral person for not eating meat? Was he morally superior to a poor Cuban family who shared their one chicken a month? Eva was not so sure.

At the end of the war, food had been scarce in Leoben. With their father gone and their mother getting sick and not knowing what was wrong with her, before her diagnosis and swift death, and the country in such a crisis, they almost never ate meat. Indeed, they didn't get enough of anything. For a while, they had rabbits. Liezel would cry when she had to take a rabbit to the butcher. But she greedily ate the meat afterward. It's true, even the death of a rabbit is a sad thing. They had tried to go to their uncle Lois's farm and get some eggs and maybe a chicken. Particularly for Liezel. She wasn't doing well at that time. Eva and Willi were okay, subsiding on broth and bread. Mushrooms picked from the mountainside. They were bigger already, stronger. They were older, they had strength. Liezel didn't.

Lois's farm that winter was not what it had been in the past. Eva remembers her mother begging. Begging him. She had wanted him to take Liezel, to let her stay there. Her mother had argued that Liezel could do some work for him, housework and farmwork, even if she was only six—and in return, just to feed her, give her milk from the cows.

Back in Leoben, the neighbors were the ones who saved Liezel from severe malnutrition. There came a time when, every night, Liezel would go to a different neighbor's house for dinner. How had her mother managed that? She was so sick then, close to the end, close to being bedridden with lupus, and then suddenly, even though it was a long illness, still, death came so suddenly. She suspected that it wasn't her mother's idea, sending Liezel around to the neighbors for meals. That it was the old woman downstairs, Frau Heller's doing. Or perhaps it had been the Schneiders, across the street from them. No matter, it saved Liezel's life.

After the war, things were going to get better. They all knew that. Their father would come home, fear and deprivation would go away. But then their father was a prisoner in France. By the time their father did return, his wife was severely ill.

She died, and he remarried. Maria.

. . .

Willi had filled her in on what happened after she moved to Vienna. Willi came to the East, once, to visit. He stayed for the day—he had business in West Berlin. It was in the late 1970s, maybe. It was long after Liezel had moved to America. Elena was at school and Hugo was dead. He sat across from her in their modest, frankly quite worn living room. She still had the house then. It was before they moved her out. Her brother, a big-boned, successful businessman, smelling strongly of Brut cologne and expensive tobacco. He brought her some delicacies—smoked fish, a bottle of cream, soft, pungent cheeses, good Austrian red wine. They ate and talked, ate and talked.

"He didn't love her, you know."

"Maria? Why marry someone you don't love?" Eva said, bile rising in her. "What can come of that?"

"So that Liezel and I would have a mother. So that someone would look after us."

"I was your mother. I looked after you." Eva felt the the blackness then, the blackness that seemed now to roll into her the way night lake water rolls over a person. Her heart pounded. Decade after decade could go by and her life so busy and troubled—how could she ever think of her past? Of that long ago, when she truly had no power? How could it still hurt?

"Yeah, but Vati thought you would get married and leave. You were so beautiful. He didn't trust you'd stay." He stroked his sister's hair. She had already started dying it. She was heavier then, too. She was a grown woman, letting her brother comfort her as if she was that young girl again, taking care of a household. Being the woman of the house.

"I would never have left." Eva knew it was true.

"Vati didn't know that." Willi looked down at his hands, where he played with some matches. "She beat us, worse than Vati did. She beat Liezel the worst. She hated Liezel. I don't know why. I was old enough, eventually, to run around and do my own thing. I was a boy. But Liezel, she had to be quiet and help in the house. If she left one speck of dirt on a plate after doing the dishes, Maria would hit her. Hit her with the switch, hit her with a spoon, and sometimes with her fists. Liezel was a walking bruise. Her nose was broken. Her arm was in a sling once. I think she was trying to run away from a beating and Maria grabbed her so hard that her elbow dislocated."

"And Vati? Where was Vati during this? He loved Liezel. He would never have let her do that. Never." Eva refused to believe these stories. Images raced in her brain, but she shook her head to rid herself of them.

"He wasn't around, Eva. That was the whole point. He couldn't be bothered. You know, I've made my peace with Maria. She was too young. I forgive her. And he didn't love her. Did you know he told her that, too, regularly? '*Ich liebe dich nichts,*' he'd say to her. How can you not feel for a woman who endured that? She had as few choices, if not fewer, than we did. She even visits me once a year or so, in Vienna. And I go out to Leoben. Not often, but I do. To say hi. She fed me dinner for years and years. I feel I owe it to her."

"You don't owe that woman anything. How can you make peace with her? She was a monster."

"We all were monsters then."

"We were children. Or you were children, I should say."

"So was she, Eva. She was a child. Not yet twenty. Think about it."

CHAPTER 20

The next morning, early, there was a knock on the door. Eva got up, bleary, she'd stayed up late, thinking, listening to music. It seemed almost impossible to get her robe on, but she managed. It was Krista.

"I have a letter for you."

"You still have my mail key?" Eva panicked. She needed her coffee. Her pills. She couldn't think.

"No, but I happened to be downstairs when the mailman came and so I told him I'd bring your letter up to you."

Eva couldn't think yet. She walked back into her room, without saying anything. Krista followed, sitting at the table. Eva poured herself a water from the sink and took her pills. Just knowing they were in her made her feel a bit better. She put water on the stove for coffee. "I can't think yet. I'm just waking up."

"I'm sorry. It's eleven already, and I thought . . ."

"You know I often sleep later," Eva interrupted. She was not pleased. She took the envelope from Krista and looked it over, to see if it had been opened. It was from Liezel. Then she looked properly at Krista. Her face wore an expression of contrition. Perhaps even of pleading. She was young and small and fragile-seeming in that moment. But Eva looked harder at her and the image of her mean and drunk, being tossed around by nasty men came clear to her. Both victim and perpetrator. It happened. Then she gathered herself. This was her neighbor. She wasn't going to make an enemy of her just now. *"Willst du einen Kaffee?"*

"Sehr gerne."

"Wie geht's deiner Mutter?"

"Ganz okay. Nicht großartig, aber okay."

Eva looked at her sternly. *"Milch und Zucker?"*

"Bitte."

For a moment, they sipped their coffees in silence. Then Eva stood up and put on her new Nina Simone record. Anything to distract from the awkwardness.

"Did you put this by my door? Someone put it by my door. I am grateful, as I wasn't here to receive it." Eva didn't mention it had been opened.

"Nein, das war nicht ich." The girl lied.

"I'm sorry, I forgot you don't like this music. I can take it off."

"No, that's not true. I mean, it's not my favorite. But don't take it off." Krista looked into her coffee cup. "Is Maggie here?"

"Yes. She's staying with Elena in Kreuzberg. But she will come visit me. I hope you'll be here and can see her."

"That would be great!" Krista's face lit up, and she nervously wiped a strand of greasy hair from her forehead. "I have so many things I want to talk to her about, about America. Maybe I could visit her someday."

Eva was startled, but tried to hide it. "Well, Krista. It's now easy to travel to America."

"Not for me. Not for people like me."

"That's not true. If you want a job there, that's different, that's harder, but to visit is not hard."

"I want a job there," the girl said grimly. "I want to move."

"I see." This was news.

"I have lived here with my mother my whole life."

"I see," Eva repeated. She was stumbling a bit now. How could Krista ask this of her, of her family, after that day? "Well, Maggie is here now. She plans to stay here for quite some time. So maybe now isn't time to talk of visiting her in America."

"She loves you and I help take care of you," Krista said, her steel eyes fixed hard on Eva. "She might help me find out how to move there, to help me, like I help you, like Elena is helping her."

"Perhaps, but people from the West are different than us," Eva said, coldly. "I love my niece, but she is a Westerner."

Eva picked up the letter again. "Thank you for bringing me my mail. It's from my sister. From Maggie's mother." Eva didn't want to read it in front of her. She wanted her to leave now, so she could read it. She went and took the needle off the record. She couldn't focus on the music. She couldn't read the letter. And now Krista talking of visiting her niece, of moving to America?

"I could read it to you," Krista offered. How her temperament changed. First the coldness, now a pleading.

"It's better I practice reading English myself, but *danke*," Eva said.

"About the other day, about Christmas . . ." Krista said, looking away.

"I won't say anything to your mother."

"I don't care so much about that. But I want you to know, I don't spend a lot of time there. With those men."

Eva looked at Krista. She could smell her dirty purple sweater. She wasn't a happy girl. Who knew what the truth was. "They don't seem like very nice people."

Krista stood and carried her coffee cup to the sink. "Thanks for the coffee. Knock on my door when Maggie is here. Or better, tell me beforehand when she is coming, if you could," she asked, betraying her desire, her vulnerability. "I want to make sure I'm here for her visit."

"*Sicher, Krista. Kein Problem*," she promised the girl as she closed the door behind her.

Eva poured more coffee, settled herself at her little table, and took out the letter.

Dear Eva,

I know it has been so long since you've heard from me. How are you? I hear that you are well from Maggie, but I would love to hear from you yourself. How is Berlin in this time of change? Exciting? Scary? Maybe a bit of both. You must enjoy that it is easier to see Elena?

Things are well here. Fred is working on a book and teaching piano. He is in relatively good health. They have some wonderful medications now. He hasn't been in the hospital in years, really. I'm wondering when we spoke last, by telephone, and fear it may have been a very long time ago. Perhaps when Maggie was in Berlin in '86? It's shocking that I don't even know. I fear I'm losing my memory already! But what can we do except bear the pain of getting older, becoming less competent in so many ways? Maybe you don't struggle with these issues. I sure do.

I am still teaching German at the Catholic school in our area. I actually am now also the head of the foreign-language department. It's been challenging, as management is not my greatest strength. But I am getting better at it as I go along. And I appreciate the challenge. It's important to keep challenging ourselves, no?

The years pass so quickly now. Perhaps you feel the same way. One thing I worry about in getting older is becoming less and less flexible, more set in my ways. I know there are things to enjoy about being at the end of our life cycle here on Earth—perhaps to look forward to a union with our Maker? Perhaps a rest from all the insanity and trouble life is? But I can't help but cling to certain aspects of youth and life—to some excitement and pleasure, to discovering new things. I am reading a lot and going to art museums, like a college girl.

You would think this all would make me accepting of Maggie and her adventurous ways, but, sadly, I can't say that it does. I am deeply worried about her. I know she respects you. I don't want to put too much pressure on you, or too many expectations, but I guess I am hoping you can keep some sort of eye on her for me. Perhaps it is too much to ask. She is a grown woman—she is not a little girl anymore. So what can any of us really do? You know that more than anything I wanted to provide my children with a great education. Something that I had to work so hard to get myself. I wanted to hand it to them. And now I wonder if that was a mistake. It was as if she used what I gave her against me, in every way. All of her knowledge she wields like weapons at me, trying to hurt me, belittle me, disagree with me on every little thing. She is shockingly rebellious, still, well past the years I was prepared to deal with rebellion. And I am without ideas on how to handle it, besides cutting her off financially, which I try to do, but then don't really do. Maybe I am weak. I know I am afraid.

Perhaps you had similar or have similar problems with Elena. I don't know. I guess I know very little about you, Eva. And it may be my fault. I should come visit. I would love for you to visit me someday. I know your feelings about America, but it's not that bad. Or at least, you could come and see for yourself, make your own decision. I would love to show you my life here.

Please call me collect if you need to, if you feel that Maggie is in danger. If she gets sick . . . anything. I'll be frank—I can't stand her boyfriend. She knows it. It's one of the reasons we don't get along right now. But I think if it wasn't Tom, it would be someone, or something else. We are just not destined to be close right now. It kills me. It does, it breaks my heart, when I'm not wrapped up in my rage for her.

I hope they are not a burden in any way. I know they are staying with Elena. Do let me know if there is anything I can do to be of help.

Busserl,

Liezel

CHAPTER 21

It had been nearly a week since Liezel's letter had arrived, but it still was strong in Eva's mind. Liezel's neat, slanted script. She wrote like their father, and like Willi. There was nothing feminine in her handwriting.

It was the first letter from her sister that hadn't been opened by others. Of course, there was Krista. But that was different, and it appeared Krista hadn't opened this letter anyway. The letter felt different than her other letters; it felt more personal. Truer. Could it be that Liezel still loved her, still loved Eva? It hardly seemed possible. They knew so little about each other's lives. They were not close.

Eva's mind was in a good place; she'd had a good week, uneventful, but good. Not too much brandy, not too many late nights, not too much leg pain. She felt almost stable, perhaps optimistic. Liezel's confiding in her had done something for her, even more than Maggie's arrival. Hans hadn't visited; normally he was the cause of her well-being. But Liezel needed her because of her daughter. It wasn't lost on Eva that Liezel's suffering and pain about her daughter were bringing Eva a kind of strength. Or that consequently, Liezel's need for Eva couldn't be an altogether good feeling for Liezel. It stemmed from her fear for Maggie, her insecurity for her daughter, and Eva comforted herself in knowing that she gave Liezel some hope, some comfort just by being in the same city as Maggie.

Liezel was getting older, but just as before, when Liezel had visited her all those years ago, Eva's image of her sister had not aged. In Eva's mind, Liezel haunted her still as a ravishing young woman, awkward and powerful in her beauty. But to have a daughter Maggie's age, she herself could not be so young anymore. Perhaps Maggie had a picture of her mother. Eva doubted it, but would ask. Maggie and Tom were coming today, for coffee and sandwiches.

Before setting out to buy good fresh bread and cheese for her visitors, Eva looked carefully in the mirror. It's not only Liezel who never ages in my mind, she thought, while touching her carefully creamed and made-up face. She saw a woman deep in middle age looking back at her, but she saw the reflection as a mask. Behind it was her true self, a young, sexual woman, a silly young woman in need of care. Behind it, was the woman she was with Hans, even the woman she was with Elena and Maggie, the woman she felt she was everywhere, really, even while at the cheese store. Especially while listening to music, wrapped in her blue robe. The reflection was nothing much—nothing more than a misleading, physical appearance.

She had offered to meet them at the train station, but they refused. Eva worried about the skinheads, and almost told them to take a roundabout way to the building, but she didn't want to make it any harder. Maggie would be with Tom. And for all the doubt that Tom inspired in people, he would most likely ward off the advances of the skinheads. Of course, it was even possible they wouldn't be there today. They were not out every day in this cold weather. And today was quite cold.

For a brief moment, Eva was ashamed of her apartment, of her room. Maggie had been there before, but she had been younger. Eva had mopped the floor, laid out a lovely embroidered Austrian tablecloth with matching napkins. The sun was shining today despite the cold; she had nothing to be ashamed of. She put on the Nina Simone record and cut bread and cheese and made coffee. She'd bought a nice bottle of red wine, too. She looked around her room—it was simple, but it was hers. And it was well tended.

They arrived, knocking on the door, Maggie saying through the closed door, "*Hallo, Tante Eva Ich bin's, die Maggie.*"

Eva had decided she could wear her robe. She opened the door somewhat grandly, swathed in the blue silk. Maggie's eyes lit up. They kissed each other's cheeks, and she shook Tom's hand and let them both in.

"They still haven't fixed the elevator, Tante Eva. Not even the new government has done that for you."

"It keeps me strong. Americans pay money to go to gyms, but all I have to do is walk up the stairs to stay healthy. "

Tom was breathing heavily.

"Are you okay, Tom? Please sit down."

"I'm fine, I'm fine. I'm just a smoker. So it takes me a minute," he said with difficulty, "to catch my breath."

Maggie looked at him with an expression that Eva couldn't quite read. It wasn't concern.

"Oh, Tante Eva, I remember this apartment so well. You look beautiful, too."

"*Setz dich, Maggie. Du bist reizend.*" Eva was touched. "Coffee?"

"Yes, please."

Eva poured the coffee and noticed her hand shaking. Surely they noticed too. But what could be done? She was nervous, excited.

"How are things? Elena tells me you've found an apartment. How wonderful."

"Yes! It's quite cheap and it gets nice light. The windows are big," she said, looking at Tom. The look Maggie gave was one Eva knew, a look for confirmation, for approval. A wariness to it. Tom did not look back at his girlfriend, but was glancing around the room with a detached interest.

"Yeah. It's great," he said, meeting Eva's eyes. his breathing much more controlled. "And I got work at a club, a great underground club. Great music. Live bands, a DJ on the other nights. In the States, I'm what they call a barback. I don't know what they call it here."

"I understand," said Eva.

"I have two interviews for teaching English this week," Maggie said. "I feel good about things. I'm sure Elena will be happy to have the place back to herself. We'll be moving out at the end of the month."

"It was her pleasure to help you out. And she appreciated the rent money. Really," Eva said.

"You're playing the record I sent you."

"Oh, yes. I play it every day. I love it so much."

"I brought you some more!" said Maggie, and picked up a bag she was carrying. "Billie Holiday's *Lady's Decca Days*. And a man named Johann Johnson, a blues singer. You like the blues, too, right, Tante Eva? Not just jazz?"

"Thank you! Yes, I'll love it all. Thank you so much."

Maggie gave Eva the records, and Eva turned them around, looking at the backs and then the front again. "I love Lead Belly. I love gospel, too. I love all Black American music." Eva laughed, hearing herself put it like that. But it was true. "Maybe I should go to America and visit your mother. And see for myself how Black people in America live. I've only seen movies about them."

"You should," Maggie said, smiling, but with some caution. Just the mention of her mother irritated her, Eva could see. "It's hard to generalize too much. There is a growing Black middle class in America. But on the other hand, one in every eight Black men has been in jail, or something awful like that."

"I wonder if you'd like rap music," said Tom. Now that

he'd settled into his chair, Eva felt she could see him better. His eyes were glassy.

"Rap music?"

"It's what the young African Americans are doing," explained Maggie. "I'm not sure what you'd think of it, actually. It's quite vulgar and violent. It's not as soul searching as the blues or jazz can be."

"African Americans?"

"Yes, that's what blacks are calling themselves."

"Not the West Indians," shot back Tom. "The West Indians prefer to call themselves Black. They're not African Americans."

"Not every Black person in America calls themselves the same thing, I suppose," Maggie said.

"Mostly, they like to call themselves 'niggas.'" Tom said wryly. "Mind if I smoke?"

"No, please smoke," Eva said, getting up to get an ashtray.

"I hate that word," Maggie said.

They were fighting, in front of her, too. It wasn't a good sign.

"Tell that to the rappers," Tom said, and lit a cigarette.

Someone knocked. "That will be my neighbor, Krista. She must hear you. Do you remember her?" asked Eva, quietly walking to the door. "She was so fond of you."

"Yes," said Maggie, nodding her head.

But it wasn't Krista. It was Hans.

"*Hans! Komm rein, bitte. Meine Nichte, Maggie und ihr Freund, Tom. Das hier ist der Hans.*"

Maggie and Tom stood, wanting to shake hands.

"*Hallo, hallo,*" Hans said, quickly, not really looking at them. He turned, as if he were leaving.

"*Warte doch! Geh nicht. Warte!*" Eva said.

"*Ich warte in meinem Auto,*" Hans said and then, to Maggie and Tom, "Nice to see you."

"Oh, Tante Eva. Is this a bad time? We can come back anytime, you know."

"No, no. I didn't know he was coming. I never know when he is coming. I'm sorry."

"No, that's fine. We'll see you soon. We want to walk around here, check out some of the squats."

"Yeah," said Tom. "A friend of mine lives near here. We were going to visit him, too."

"That's so nice you have a friend around here," Eva said, with relief.

Maggie hugged her. Her niece smelled sweet, like vanilla. She said, "I'll call you. We'll go to Café Einstein. Do you remember going there with me? We won't be able to sit in the garden, because it's too cold. But it would be fun to go back there."

"Yes, yes," said Eva, but she wasn't really paying attention. She could only think of Hans, downstairs, waiting for her.

When she got downstairs, she looked for his old car, but then she saw the Cadillac. She felt bad for hurrying Maggie and Tom out and for not inviting Krista as she'd promised. Hans leaned over the expanse of car and opened the door for her, from inside. *"Komm,"* he said. *"Wir fahren nach Wandlitz."*

"Wie lange? Kann ich etwas mitnehmen?"

"Nein, nein. Wir haben keine Zeit. Komm."

She didn't ask where Paula and the kids were. She had her purse with her pills, and she had grabbed the present for Hans. Hans was always in a hurry, often for no reason. But that was okay. He would maybe buy her something then, she thought, giddily. A new toothbrush. A sweater.

The drive was lovely. They were warm in the car, the sun shining brightly on the windows. Eva looked at Hans: he was calm, happy.

Wandlitz was a suburb of Berlin, about a forty-minute drive if there was no traffic. Built by the Party for the well connected, it was really one big neighborhood of similar two-story houses, with, at the time they were built, state-of-the-art kitchens, good heat, and most of all, privacy. Nestled in the thick woods, each house was nearly invisible from the far end of its driveway. Built in the early 1960s, it had once had a guard twenty-four hours a day at the entrance, and East German military men drove around the quiet neighborhood, guns hanging out of their windows. They drove slowly, looking left and right, in their thick gray uniforms, their loaded arms shining with a yellow fluorescent band.

Now, the area had faded some, Eva noted as they entered. It seemed quiet. She had heard that many people had left. Many people had left Berlin and the East in general. And so many others from farther East had arrived. But not here—no immigrants had made it out here.

Hans clearly still lived here. He had taken her here once for an entire week, years and years ago. They were very much in love then. They were new together. Paula had been gone for two weeks. He didn't feel the need to try to be secretive about her. Why try? Everybody knew everything. It was the way things were then. And yet they had been somewhat discreet. During Eva's stay there, she almost never left the house. No one saw her. He brought her things. Once, they went to the private restaurant of Wandlitz. Beef stroganoff, wonderful, buttery spaetzle. Chocolate cake. One of the most wonderful meals she'd ever had. They didn't touch once, though she had wanted to. She tried to put her foot on his, under the table, but he had pulled away. It was enough that they were out together. Discreet, but not trying to fool anyone. Who didn't have a mistress?

Inside, the house smelled airless and stale, as if no one had been there for a while. Hans put down his car keys on a table in the hallway and lit a cigarette.

"Bring mir ein Bier. Du weißt noch, wo die Küche ist, no?"

"Ja, sicher." Eva took off her shoes first and rubbed her feet for a moment. She padded quietly into the kitchen; it hadn't changed at all. The same refrigerator, the same stove. The same counter tops. She opened the fridge and took out two bottles of beer, then looked for glasses. She didn't remember which cabinet they were in but found them shortly. The

glasses seemed dusty, so she rinsed them out before pouring the beer into them.

"*Danke, Schatzi,*" he said as she brought him the beer and leaned over and kissed him.

"Do you live here still?" Eva asked. "It seems as if you don't."

"We are in the process of moving. Paula has taken the kids already to Poland. I still have business here, and I always will. I'll be here often. Very often. But we won't need this big house. I'll maybe find a small flat or stay at a nice hotel. You'll like that, Schatzi, won't you? And I have my cabin." He finished his beer quickly. "So many things have changed. Are changing. I'm not leaving for at least six months. Or so I think. I can't know for sure." He turned to her, and stroked her face, her neck.

"Don't leave me, Hansi. Don't leave." She did like the idea of the hotel in the moment—its lack of permanence. Or even a flat that was just his. Strangely, she felt the idea of Paula permanently away was a threat to her. The change—the endless upheaval. But that was why he was so quiet. That was why he seemed so calm. He had this secret. He was always calmest when he had a secret from her.

"I'm not leaving for at least six months, I just told you. Maybe longer. And Paula is gone the entire time. So it will be just us." He wrapped his huge body around hers, squeezing her tightly. She felt soft under his arms, like a cushion for him.

"You'll come often, to visit me?"

Hans took a long drag of his cigarette and crushed it in an ashtray. He was smoking Marlboro Reds, which he never smoked. A Cadillac, now American cigarettes. He had often smoked cigarettes from the West, but German ones, either Davidoff or West. "I'll be here on business every month. We'll see each other when I can."

Eva began to cry. Business was always first, like Hugo and his art. Why couldn't he just say, "*Doch*, I'll come to see you."

"No crying, Eva."

She stood and looked out the large windows. The windows had not aged, didn't seem dated or fragile with the years. They were made of thick glass, with beautiful black metalwork. And they seemed recently cleaned, too. Outside, the trees were thin black lines, crossing each other endlessly, making a dense web. Snow lay on the ground, white and unharmed. "Make love to me," she asked, quietly, and put down her beer.

Later, when the evening light had faded completely in the bedroom, Hans stood up and said, "Follow me."

Eva wanted to stay in bed. "What?"

"I have to show you something. I want to give you something."

"Can't it wait until tomorrow? I have a Christmas gift for you, too."

"It's not a Christmas gift."

He walked ahead of her, naked except for slippers, and then he took two robes out of the closet in the bedroom. *"Hier. Zieh das an."*

Reluctantly, Eva put on the robe. It smelled of mildew. *"Wo gehen wir?"*

"Downstairs. It's colder down there."

It was dark. Eva held on to Hans's robe in front of her as they went down the steep stairs. Hans tried to get the light to turn on, but the bulb was out. *"Scheiße,"* he said, and then he fumbled around in a box and switched on a flashlight. *"Komm,"* he said. *"Schau."*

On a wooden shelf, next to a can of paint, were two small glass jars with yellow pieces of cloth inside of them.

"What? What is this?"

Hans shone the light on the jars. "See," he said, and Eva looked at him, smiling there at her. "Look! Look at the jars. Don't look at me, you silly woman."

On the jars were white labels. One said HUGO HERMANN; the other said EVA STILLER HERMANN.

"They're your smells. Your smells were bottled. So we could track you if we needed to. Hugo had many subversive friends, Wolf Biermann, Vera Lengsfeld. It was the way things were done." Eva looked at Hans. He had a wistful expression, thoughtful. And then he turned to her with a look of pride. "I brought you yours, and Hugo's. I took them for you."

She had always known he was Stasi. She just didn't like to

think about it. And what was he now? Maybe it was time she stopped wanting not to know. Eva picked up the jars carefully. Wolf Biermann. Vera Longsfeld. Her Hugo. Ghosts, all of them. She said, "They won't fit in my purse."

"I'll give you a bag, Schatzi," he said. Eva's eyes had adjusted to the dark. Hans stood there, his face regal with power and kindness.

"Is that what was in those boxes at the lake house?" She hadn't wanted to ask; it just came out. Eva winced, unnecessarily. He put a hand on her arm, somewhat gently. It was a relief.

"Don't you worry about those boxes, Schatzi. In fact, pretend you never saw them."

CHAPTER 22

Hugo had been devastated when Wolf Biermann left. But no one was surprised. By that time, many artists were tired of how things were, of the constant surveillance, of how disappointing the government was, of how they'd become the opposite of what they had promised to be. The lack of goods didn't help, nor did the fact that they had things better than the vast majority of the population and even then, they didn't have the things they wanted. Desire for good things or a good life were seen as capitalist, as greedy. People were confused; they wanted, but they were ashamed of their desires. And was that such a bad thing? Eva thought shame had its purpose. When she occasionally looked at American magazines—*People*, *Vanity Fair*, *Glamour*—she was often disgusted. It was too much. To have some shame was not a bad thing.

Of course East Germany had its problems, but airing frustration—for which Wolf was known in his work—was considered just plain heretical. Communism was the religion, the only real religion allowed. Wolf was lucky to get out safely. Others had tried to escape. People had disappeared. But Eva didn't like to think about those things. Not then, not now for the most part, but now, *now*, she knew that it was cowardly of her.

They had Wolf and Greta and their daughter Nina over before they left. At that point, Hugo knew that his house must be bugged. But what did it matter? He felt he had nothing to hide. He knew he would die a fairly loyal Communist, die there in East Germany. He knew it from the moment that Eva and he arrived. What did it matter that the Stasi, the government, wanted to hear him fuck Greta—or his own wife, for that matter—listening to scratchy, barely audible tapes? Sometimes, he did complain, mildly, to Eva. But never to Wolf or the other disgruntled intellectuals. Around them, he was often quiet and even sometimes defensive of the GDR. This was the country that had saved him from the Nazis! This was the country that educated all of its people, where no one was hungry. No one was without a home or without an education, and everyone got excellent health care. Yet he knew there were things wrong. As the years wore on, the problems became obvious, often painfully so.

"What a waste of human effort, of the short time we have here on this planet. Just a useless folly," he had sighed, looking older than usual in bed next to her. Eva stroked his coarse hair. His hair was dry, brittle even, now that his gray hair had turned white. "Forcing Wolf to leave. Spending all this time and energy eavesdropping, collecting useless information, and then filing it properly. As if having proper files matters when the information is utterly useless."

Eva remembered this as she contemplated the jars of smells in the bag. Hugo would say, "To think what this country could be like if the money and time and energy were used in other ways. It's a tragedy."

Eva had said nothing. What country *wasn't* a tragedy? They had made their bed here, and now they would lie in it. Eva didn't believe that anywhere else was better. Just different. She stroked his hair until he fell asleep and then, content, she slept, too.

Later she realized Hugo missed Greta more than Wolf when they both defected. She could tell when he missed a woman, when one of his affairs ended. He paced slowly around the house and stopped taking pictures. He drank too much coffee. He even became grumpy and short tempered with Elena. And yet, he became very kind and needy toward Eva.

"*Bitte, Liebchen, würdest du mir einen Kaffee machen?*" he'd ask, his eyes a bit droopy and guiltridden.

"*Sicher. Kommt gleich,*" she'd answer, grateful for his neediness. It was a happy time for Eva. He would always turn to her. Until, of course, he started seeing Mausi. By then, he didn't turn to anyone, really. It was just the two women, circling a dying man. He never had to ask for anything.

CHAPTER 23

Maggie and Tom were moving the next day. Elena had called her mother and suggested they all go to Café Einstein together that night, to celebrate the couple's moving into their own apartment.

Eva was carefully putting on makeup. Bright rouge, mascara. She sprayed herself with perfume, with her 4711. She was wearing the red dress Hansi gave her. On the record player was the Billie Holiday record. She was trying to give it a chance. It hadn't moved her yet, not like the Nina Simone records. Her voice was too thin, and the songs seemed light in comparison. But she knew she needed to listen to her more, give the woman some time. A knock on the door startled her. Could it be Hans? She couldn't disappoint Maggie again. She opened the door and saw Krista, a sheepish expression on her pale face, in her purple metallic sweater. She smelled strongly. It is the sweater, thought Eva. She can't bear to take it off, to part with it long enough to wash it.

"*Hallo, Eva.*"

"*Hallo, Krista. Was ist los?*" Eva decided to get straight to the point. She didn't want to be late. She liked Café Einstein. She hadn't been there in so long, perhaps not since Maggie was in Berlin in 1986. It had a beautiful garden, but it would be too cold to enjoy it. Regardless, it was a lovely cafe; it reminded her of the cafés of Vienna.

"My mother would like to talk with you, if you have a moment." She didn't look at Eva.

"Well, I am about to go out." Eva felt trapped. "What time is it?" She looked frantically at the wall clock. She had plenty of time. Over an hour before she had to be there. "I have time, I have time."

She followed Krista into her apartment. It had been many months since she'd seen Krista's mother. And since she'd seen Krista with the skinheads, she'd been dreading seeing her. It was as if she were lying to the woman, not telling her what she knew about her daughter.

The apartment was slightly bigger than Eva's but it seemed even smaller, perhaps because two people lived there. Krista's mother sat in an orange armchair, a radio on next to her. She didn't seem to notice Eva come in, her eyes were so filmy. She was even heavier now than the last time Eva had seen her, her skin waxy and her neck all folds. She was mostly bald. The sight of her upset Eva, as had been the case for years, which was why she never visited. Shame came over her. This poor woman. And then she thought, and poor Krista, to have to live watching her mother deteriorate, to live looking at this woman. Life was cruel. She thought about something Hansi one said to her: "There are no winners, just survivors."

"Frau Hermann, kommen Sie herein! Danke, dass Sie sich die Zeit für mich nehmen." She gestured for Eva to come in.

"Ich warte in deiner Wohnung auf dich, Eva. Ist das okay?" said Krista as she backed out of the apartment. Eva looked around. Things did not seem very clean and she was nervous about her dress. She didn't want to get it dirty. She settled on a plastic-covered kitchen chair across from Gabi after brushing it off with her hand.

"Sit down! Sit down!" Gabi said.

"I am sitting, thank you!"

"Ach, my eyes are not so good anymore. First the back and then the legs, now the eyes and ears. It is one thing after another. Thank God for my Krista. I would be dead without her."

"You're very lucky to have such a devoted daughter," Eva said. This was true. Whatever else Eva thought of Krista, or worried about her, really, she was devoted to her mother. Although she should keep their apartment cleaner.

"How is your daughter? Your Elena?"

"Very well, thank you."

"And I hear your niece Maggie from America is visiting Berlin again."

"Yes, she is. She is here to stay, in fact, indefinitely." There was a pause. Eva felt her face color. "In fact, I am going to see her tonight. Perhaps Krista would like to come?"

"I know she'd be delighted to. She remembers the visit with

her so well. You know how young people are, obsessed with America, and everything American. But I don't mean to sound disparaging. Your niece was so sweet to Krista. They are about the same age, and . . ." Frau Haufmann stopped, breathing heavily from the effort of talking.

"She's welcome to come. We are all meeting at a café. Maggie is here with her boyfriend, Tom, also an American. And my daughter will be there also. Maggie and Tom were staying with Elena and have just found their own apartment. So we are celebrating, you see."

"Are you sure it's a convenient time for Krista to join you?"

"Yes, yes. *Kein Problem.*"

"But this is not why I asked to talk with you," she said, lowering her voice. Frau Haufmann rubbed her hands together nervously; they made a rasping noise. Eva noticed that her neck was also lined with dirt. Why wasn't she properly bathed? Her irritation at Krista grew. And then she wondered how much longer this would go on, the slow spiral downward. Her health, her everything. She thought of Hugo. No one can know how long. How long did it take Hugo? Even when she remembered more of less the amount of months, there was nothing exact. The time of demise is a warped time, endless and nothing.

"No? *Über etwas anderes?*"

"No. Well, no. But I did want to talk about Krista. She thinks so much of you. She enjoys having you as a neighbor."

Eva thought of Krista, angry and mean, the things she'd

said about her that night. And yet, now, seeing her contrite and sheepish while asking Eva to come over and speak to her mother. She was still a child really, and behaved like one. But she was in a woman's body now, and when she'd been cruel, she'd shown something else, something like the black liquid that Eva knew existed not only in herself.

"I enjoy having you both as my neighbors as well. Krista is often so helpful, getting my mail for me, for instance."

"She likes to get your mail for you. She does." Again, Frau Haufmann rubbed her hands together. And then, in a very low voice, "I am worried that I am too much of a burden for her."

"I think she is proud that she takes such good care of you." Eva looked at the old woman. She couldn't be that much older than Eva herself, and yet she was so close to death. Her rheumy eyes betrayed little emotion, but her mouth was held tightly, her neck bent.

"She will get my apartment when it is my time to go."

"Oh, Frau Haufmann! You are not going anywhere."

Frau Haufmann smiled. "But as you know, this neighborhood is not what it used to be. I worry for her."

"She's young and bright and will make a good life for herself," Eva said firmly. "You shouldn't worry about her."

"I am worried about her. This is what I wanted to say. I don't see well. I don't hear well. And Krista doesn't talk to me like she did a few years ago. But she is all right? You think she is all right?"

"She is fine," Eva said, and it came out easily. The lie. It was her job to protect Frau Haufmann, not worry her. "Don't worry about your daughter. Take care of yourself." It was true. The young, no matter how crazy and messed up, would almost always be fine. They had time on their side. Eva patted the old woman's hand and stood up.

In the taxi, on the way to Café Einstein, Krista sat huddled against the door, decidedly away from Eva. Eva didn't call anyone to let them know she was bringing Krista. For some reason, she felt she was failing Maggie again. As she had failed her when she and Tom came to visit, and she left with Hansi. But she tried to reason with herself. She wasn't disappearing this time. She was just bringing someone who was, essentially, uninvited.

Krista faced out the window. She was trying not to smile. Well, it was making the girl happy, so God must be pleased. Eva closed her eyes for a minute and said a silent prayer: Thank you, God, for making this lost soul happy. Please show her the way to You.

"Does Maggie know I'm coming?" Krista asked, still looking out the window. It was a splurge, taking a taxi. Eva felt pretty and special in her dress. But she was also hoping that Maggie would pay for the drinks. Or Elena. And now that Krista was coming along, she felt even more worried about this. She would have to pay for something, now that she brought an extra person along.

"No. But she'll be happy to see you."

"My mother made you bring me," Krista said, and now looked at Eva. Her eyes were shining. She had a fine nose, and although her hair was dirty, it was thick and healthy. Her mouth seemed pinched today, like her mother's, and it was this perhaps that made her not so attractive seeming. She had a gorgeous mouth, but she held it poorly, with so much tension, all screwed up. This, and not wearing any makeup. A little color would make her look nice. Eva thought she should maybe offer to make up Krista's face.

"Your mother did no such thing. I offered to bring you. I'm only sorry it took this long for you to see Maggie. I know how much it meant to you, to see her."

"My father was in America."

"Really? I never knew your father."

"He was there for the Olympics. A shot-putter."

"How wonderful!"

"He died of heart failure when I was very young. He had been given so many steroids. They killed him." Krista's smile was gone and her eyes turned dark. The blackness.

Eva looked away from Krista's face. And truthfully, she was stunned. She'd been neighbors with these people for a decade and yet she never knew this? Frau Haufmann, Gabi, kept to herself, mostly, of course. Perhaps when they both moved in, they had shared that they were widows, but that's it. Eva turned back to Krista and said, "Well, that was an unfortunate and a terrible thing the government did. But they didn't know. They didn't know that the steroids had any side effects. I'm very sorry to hear about your father. His passing must have been hard on your family."

Krista smiled. "It was so long ago. I barely remember him. But I do remember the pictures of America."

"I'm sure you saw pictures of America in school as well. Pictures of the dark side of America, of the South Side of Chicago, where all the Black people live in poverty."

"Yes, but my father had pictures of America that made it look so beautiful."

"I'm sure parts of it are."

"When my mother dies, I am going to go. I want to visit Utah. And Florida. And California."

Who could blame her for thinking ahead? For wanting to be free. The shame came over Eva again. Shame and blackness, pouring over her at their own will, as if Eva had no control, as if mystery were real. Which it was, she knew; she knew of forces beyond her.

Krista, despite her troubles, had so often been kind and helpful. It was true that she'd lately grown sullen, even angry. That she was changing. That she was hanging out with skinheads. But for years, she was only good. How long can goodness last? We are all humans, thought Eva, all troubled. "I should visit your mother more often. I enjoyed speaking with her today."

Krista made a sort of noise, a *huumph*. She looked away again.

"You know," said Eva, "Maggie is here because she doesn't like America."

"Well, of course she doesn't. No one knows what they have until they lose it. And I'm not saying there aren't problems with America. I just want to see them for myself. I want to be able to know what it's like with my own eyes. And whatever the problems are, they can't be worse than things are here," she said, grimly.

Eva didn't know what to say. She'd had plenty of chances to go, but Krista must know that. But why go to America, when America had already come here, to Western Europe, which had now come to her Eastern Europe, littering its sacred boulevards with McDonald's and outlet clothing stores? Of course, Eva loved the outlet clothing stores, filled to bursting with lovely, cheaply made clothes from Asia. She loved going to them, running her fingers through the endless racks of soft and colorful clothing. She loved them, but she felt they were wrong, too. And if she were to be honest with herself, prior to the Wall coming down, the clothes available from the USSR and Romania were just as cheaply made. And not as beautiful. And more expensive.

The taxi swerved down the boulevard that led to Café Einstein. It was a dark, long boulevard, wide and curving. Suddenly, a woman with short bleached hair and tall shiny boots opened a fur coat at them. The taxi's headlights brightly illuminated her white, naked body. It glowed at them, abruptly, like a light being thrust on. Eva gasped. Krista, too, had her mouth open in surprise. And then there were many. A parade of patent leather boots and fur coats and exotic, barely existent lingerie. Black, white, and Asian women. Groups of them smoking and talking, and single loners, lurching toward the taxi, their breasts bared.

There was something so beautiful about these women to Eva. Their skin seemed perfectly taut and creamy smooth. The bright colors—the dyed white or red hair, the shiny black boots that looked like fresh wet paint up to their thighs, the red lace bra that revealed rouged nipples against white skin—they were the colors any little girl or little boy would salivate over at a candy store. They were all licorice and peppermints and and chocolate bars to Eva. Her face colored and her breath quickened. How could she, a God-fearing woman, a woman who prayed every day, lust after these whores, or rather, desire to be like them? Lust is in all of our hearts, thought Eva. God knows it and helps us struggle with it.

A pang of jealousy seared her chest. Did her Hansi go to whores? Why wouldn't he? That was what it was all about. She just wanted to be his object of desire.

"Das ist nicht richtig," said the taxi driver, in his heavily accented German. He was from somewhere east, perhaps Poland or the Ukraine, judging by his accent. *"Ein Auto könnte sie anfahren. Sie darf nicht so dicht rankommen."*

It was true, they came out at the cars so quickly, so stealthily, and they came close. It was dangerous.

"Das sind Huren," said Krista, her face clouding over. "They get what's coming to them."

"Vielleicht," said the taxi driver, "but I don't want my

car damaged. I don't want to get in an accident because of them."

They stopped at a light. A Black woman in red boots walked up to the cab and leaned down toward the window, to where Eva and Krista sat. Krista opened the window and screamed, *"Hure! Geh weg! Dreckschwein!"*

"Krista, bitte nicht." Eva leaned over the girl to roll up the window. The woman turned away, unfazed. How many times had people spoken to her this way? Many times, every day, for most of her life, thought Eva. "Krista, that's no way to speak to anyone."

The cab driver laughed. Krista said, "They come here and ruin our country."

"They come here because they have very few choices. Or worse, they are forced to, against their will."

Krista looked at Eva. "I'm surprised you make excuses for them. But that is how you are. Always kind," she said, but not with any kindness on her part.

"I can feel for the unfortunate. So can you. So can anyone."

Krista laughed in Eva's face, leaning in too close and Eva pushed away from the girl. It was too aggressive, too mean. Eva could smell her so strongly. Then she abruptly turned her head away from Eva. Eva felt herself harden and she didn't fight it.

"You should wash that sweater, Krista," Eva said. "It smells terrible."

Krista turned back to Eva, her face changed. The girl was

mercurial beyond belief. One moment all demon, then a startled innocent. *"Wie bitte?"*

"Wirklich," Eva said, and plugged her nose with her fingers.
"Du riechst schlecht."

Inside the café, the atmosphere was quiet, even serene. Krista
seemed a bit cowed and Eva was pleased. She'd been a child
who needed a quick slap on the back of the head, and Eva felt
fine in giving it to her. Beethoven played, not too loudly, not
too softly, in the background. The lights were soft and yellow,
and the long, elegant room was warm. Eva stroked her dress
where it lay on her shoulders, silky and cool, and glanced
around. They were the first to arrive, and she had been worried about being late. Luckily, there were still some tables big
enough to accommodate the entire group. She ushered Krista
over to one, not too far from the door but far enough so as not
to catch a cold breeze when it opened. It was the perfect table,
really.

Krista ordered a beer and Eva just ordered a brandy and
water—which she calculated she would need to make last
most of the night; perhaps she could have one more drink,
but just one—when the others came in.

They were a bit loud to Eva's ears. Loud Americans. She
loved her niece, but hearing her come in laughing and talking
to Tom made her wince. Her daughter loped behind them. As
they came gliding toward the table, Eva thought, they are so
young! They were full of themselves, and the future. They

were moist with possibility and arrogance and foolishness. For a moment, Eva envied them, and was proud of them, too.

As everyone settled around the small table, Eva noticed that Maggie and Tom seemed off balance, distracted, as if they were high on something. Eva remembered how Hugo's friends sometimes smoked hashish, how strange they behaved, how spacey and blissful they'd become. Maggie looked fairly terrible. And she was such a beautiful girl! Maggie's makeup caked unattractively on her cheeks, unsuccessfully hiding dark purple spots. Her fingers moved quickly and too expressively. Her whole face seemed to move in exaggerated ways. Eva tried to squash her worry and quickly drank down her brandy. She would just have to have one more. She was nervous, worried.

"I've brought Krista with me," Eva said, standing and embracing first Maggie, then Elena. "Maggie, you remember Krista? I wrote to you, too, how eager she was to see you again."

Krista gave Eva a quick glare. Eva had embarrassed her. She was just doing her best.

"And my daughter Elena. And Tom," Eva added. Everyone shook hands somewhat awkwardly.

Maggie said, "It's so nice to see you again. How are you?"

Maggie's eyes drooped, but her voice was lively. This comforted Eva some. How bad could things be, if her voice sounded so upbeat? Beers were ordered. Everyone was seated.

"I'm doing well. Much has changed since you were last

here, and for the most part, I think the changes will be good for everyone." Her English was so good. Nearly flawless. "But it's hard, too, this time of transition. My mother is hanging in there. But how are you? You are here indefinitely? That's exciting, no?"

"Yes. We couldn't be more thrilled to be here. I'm teaching already, teaching English at a small language institute near the Ku'damm. I have mostly non-German students. And we have an apartment." At this, they all clinked glasses. "I'm shocked at the rapid changes, too, so I can imagine how you must feel. I remember your mother had health problems. The East was so good at taking care of their people. Tom and I are a bit dismayed to see how quickly the GDR has become impotent politically, or socially, really. We worry about its former people. You. You, Eva." Maggie looked at Eva. Eva caught her glance and tried to hold it. This was the first time the girl had looked at her, having evaded eye contact from the time she entered.

"Don't worry about me, Maggie, Liebchen," Eva said, hearing the sternness in her voice and feeling the warmth of the brandy. "Worry about yourself."

At this, there was some silence. Tom lit a cigarette and seemed to examine Krista as he blew smoke off to the side.

"I think everyone should worry about me, now that I have no one helping me with the rent," Elena said, making everyone laugh. She was good at that. At distracting, at drawing away from an ugly issue. It was clearly a gift with many uses.

"So tell me about your new apartment," Eva said.

"It's perfect," Tom answered. "It's actually not far from you, Eva. It's in the former GDR. It's big. It's a bit derelict, but I'm handy around the house. I know how to fix things." He grinned and lit another cigarette. "And, of course, it's very affordable." Eva noticed something about the way he talked. The understatement. The choice of words. It reminded her of the people for whom she worked in Vienna, all those years ago. People with money. Never is anything "cheap"; rather, it's affordable. Never is a place a dump; it's "a bit derelict." Yes, he was from money. It made her trust him all the less.

"You already have a lit cigarette, Tom," Eva said.

He glanced at the ashtray. "Well, I guess I do!"

Krista picked it up and knocked off a long, gray ash. "I'll smoke it," she said, and began to do so. Maggie was staring off into space, her mouth hanging open. Her eyes started to close. She was nodding off.

"Maggie?" Eva asked.

"Don't worry about her," said Tom, stretching his legs under the table. For a moment, Eva felt his shoe on hers. She immediately pulled back. It wasn't meant for her, though. That was for sure. Krista, sitting next to her, began smiling shyly and stretching her neck. Eva had never noticed, but it was a beautiful neck—white and long, the opposite of her mother's. Someday, thought Eva, her neck will be gone, like everything else. "Maggie's very tired," Tom went on. "We've been packing all day. And you know how meticulous your niece is. She worked very hard to put everything in the right box, and then labeled the boxes appropriately. She's got those Austrian organizational genes." He laughed, looking at Krista, who laughed as well, as if on command, to please him. Eva's skin warmed even more.

"Poor thing," Eva said. "She doesn't look well. And I'm her aunt. I'm supposed to look after her."

"She was packing all day," Elena added, to comfort her mother. "Unlike this one," she added, gesturing to Tom.

"Hey, that kind of work is for the ladies," he said, smiling widely. He was always smiling, thought Eva. And it never seemed nice.

"*Noch eine Runde!*" Elena said, raising her arms boisterously. "*Und die geht auf mich!*"

The waiter, dressed formally in black and white, came somewhat hurriedly to the table. He didn't like the noise, Elena's outburst. It was a quiet cafe, bohemian yes, but not seedy. He must have disliked the whole table. Eva folded her hands in her lap, looking down at her bright, shiny dress. The waiter probably didn't like her, either. Her heart sank.

"*Noch eine Runde, bitte!*" said Elena, raising her arms as if she were conducting the Beethoven that played on. Always mocking, always making fun. "*Wir haben durst! Wir haben Durst!*"

After the waiter brought them drinks, Eva felt braver; just seeing the drink in front of her helped. "Tom, what are you doing for work?" Eva asked.

He raised an eyebrow at Eva and was about to speak when Maggie woke and interrupted. "He's going to fix up our apartment. That will be worth a lot. We pay very little rent because he's going to make it up to code for the landlord. And we can live off of my salary."

"I'm not a huge fan of regular jobs," said Tom, with that greasy smile on his face. "That's why we were excited to leave the States, the land of hard work and no benefits, a country that doesn't take care of its people."

Krista said, "But at least there is opportunity there. There is so little opportunity here."

Tom leaned toward her, saying, "The opportunities in the US just propagate materialism, just create the illusion of needing things no one actually needs." He lit a cigarette off of his old one and then stubbed out the butt. "All we need is food and shelter. Everything else is a mirage." At this he fluttered a hand toward the ceiling.

Maggie sat up now. "What about love?"

Tom squeezed Maggie's shoulder, saying, "Love? Another capitalist invention."

For some reason, everyone at the table thought that it was funny except for Eva. Eva felt a sharp irritation rise in her.

"Can I have a cigarette, Tom?" If he was so antimaterialistic, he could part with his cigarettes, she thought.

"Of course, Eva," Tom said and then, in his mocking gallant way, offered her the pack.

"Marlboros. Western cigarettes," she said.

"As much as I love Berlin," Tom said, "your tobacco is terrible." He lit Eva's cigarette with a gold-toned lighter.

"What a beautiful lighter," Eva remarked.

"Thank you," Tom said. "It was my grandfather's," he said, carefully pocketing it.

Of course it was, thought Eva, but she just smiled at him.

CHAPTER 24

The next morning, Eva's legs hurt her badly for the first time in what seemed like months. They throbbed and burned. And her head hurt, too. She had had too much brandy the night before and ended up smoking cigarettes, too. She lifted the shade. The sun was bright and she immediately squinted her eyes closed and sat back down. Next to her bed were her bottles of pills and a glass of water. At least she'd had the presence of mind to set things up for the morning. She reached over and swallowed her morning pills. The water felt good on her parched throat and she slowly drank the whole glass, her hand shaking a bit, before resting her head back on the pillow. In a little while, the pills would kick in. And then she would get up. She looked at the clock—it was nearly noon. She closed her eyes, and when she opened them again, her heart was pounding and her mouth was very dry. It was time to rise.

She put on her robe, used the bathroom, and drank more water while she fixed the coffee. Half the day was over and she was glad. This was not a day she wanted to wake to. Her niece was on drugs, her niece's boyfriend was playing footsie with Krista, and as of today, they were all neighbors. Ideally, Eva would be happy that Maggie was living nearby. But she was a mess, one Eva felt responsible for. This had never been one of Eva's strengths—taking care of troubled people. She had a heart for them, but not the capacity for the work it took to get them out of trouble. She had to get rid of Tom, but Eva knew very well how little could be done about that. If a woman loves a man, the more desperate things are, the more desperately she'll cling to him. It appeared that Maggie loved him, from her letters, from the way she behaved when Eva first saw them, right off the plane. One hope that Eva held was that Maggie was young enough and wise enough to change. Also, Eva didn't think her neighborhood was very safe or pretty. She herself wasn't ashamed to live here. She was an East German, whatever that meant now. But everyone new who moved into the neighborhood was either a poor immigrant or a troubled youth. The skinheads. The pale girls dressed in black, coughing loudly and hollowly as they walked the nearly desolate streets.

Maggie was a woman now. One with troubles, like most people. What did Eva think she could do? She could talk to Maggie, but she feared making things worse. Confrontation almost never works, Eva felt certain. It had never worked for her or for anyone she knew. One had to come around to the truth oneself. She would call Elena. Elena should have called me, thought Eva, should have told me what was going on. And yet, Eva had known. Why should Elena call and tell her something they all knew but didn't talk about? She was just trying to share some of the responsibility with Elena. Her own daughter, to help with the daughter of her sister.

And so, then there was Liezel. What should she say to Liezel? Anything? Would that be betraying Maggie? Or taking care of her?

She ran herself a very warm bath and, after pinning her hair back, slathered her face with cold cream.

She felt responsible for the world, and she resented that. Who took care of *her*? Even Krista, with her getting the mail, and helping out here and there, had become a burden. Oh, how her legs hurt! Hopefully, the bath would help. And resting. Yes, today, she would just rest.

She shut off the bath when it was full and walked over to her record player, her legs both weirdly numb and painful with each step. The little bit of brandy she put in her coffee was kicking in. She'd needed it this morning, to calm her nerves and to help with the pain. Later, maybe she'd find a bottle of codeine. That would really help. She tried not to take codeine often, though. If she took it too much, it stopped working well. There had been times when it stopped working, so she took more and more. It had scared her. She didn't want to accidentally kill herself.

The Billie Holiday album was still on the record player. The water was very warm, and even though her legs went hot when they gave her trouble, she knew the warm water would feel good on them. Relax them, even cool them off a bit, as if the warmth from the bath pulled out the heat from her legs. She looked down at her naked body—her large hips, her round stomach. Self-consciously, she put her hands on her still shapely breasts and looked farther down herself. Her legs had red blotches running along them, and her ankles looked swollen. Her legs had always been nice—not too skinny, like Liezel's, but not thick like trees. She hated to see them look like this. Perhaps it was time to see a doctor again. Even though she'd been a nurse, she hated seeing doctors. They so rarely had anything useful to say or do. Of course, her prescriptions were important to her, but she could hardly credit any doctor for that. She sank into the water and breathed deeply.

Billie Holiday sang in the other room, and Eva could hear her well. The fourth song on the record was her favorite. There were many good songs, "Solitude," "The Man I Love," "God Bless the Child." The upbeat "All of Me." But "Long Gone Blues" was the best. It was, in many ways, the only real blues song on the record, Billie Holiday singing how she'd been her man's slave since she'd been his babe, but before she'd be his dog, she'd see him in his grave.

Yes, this was the blues. This was some sort of truth, perhaps the ugly truth. It wasn't dressed up to be something else. And yet even on this song, Holiday sounded distant, even antiseptic. Eva thought maybe it was the recording, that the way it was recorded rendered the music too clean and distant. But Maggie was right, Holiday was good. Beneath the recording was a glimmer of heart, of pain.

Maggie. What was Eva to do? She'd write Liezel. And then, just try to stay in her life. Maybe, Eva thought guiltily, try to make herself more available. She'd been so looking forward to Maggie arriving, but now that she was here and here indefinitely, there was no real hurry to see her. There was always the next day and the day after that, and so on. When she was here just for that summer, it had been different. The distinct parameters of the visit had lent an urgency to her time here. Eva closed her eyes and sank deeper into the tub. And Maggie had been so young then. Still so trusting and innocent. The difference between a teenager who still lived at home and a woman in her twenties who'd lived away was huge. Eva tried to feel the desire to protect her niece, but instead her heart filled with fear, with dread. She breathed deeply. She had poured an oil in the bath, scented with melissa. A short, sharp pain jabbed her forehead and she sat up.

Holiday sang that she was a good girl, but her love was all wrong. Eva started rubbing her legs furiously, and it felt good. It was about circulation. She just needed to improve her circulation. That's why making love to Hans always helped. That's why walking over to Maggie's new home would be good. She'd do it, soon. Maybe even without calling first. But first, she'd write her sister.

CHAPTER 25

Dear Liezel,

As you know, Maggie has a job and an apartment (which I haven't visited yet but will very soon), and in many ways, she overwhelms me with her maturity and her responsible nature. I think she got a job teaching within two weeks of being here. The apartment hunting took a bit longer, which was fine with Elena. In fact, I think Elena will miss the company. She pretends to like her artistic solitude, but really she's a boisterous, social person who liked having them around more than she'd admit. They also helped her with the rent. Did you know that? And Elena greatly appreciated that. She doesn't make much selling her work or handling Hugo's estate and occasionally picks up work at a friend's tavern. Of course, she also gets some money from the government. Even in West Germany, they support their artists. And she's gotten some grants. She is doing well.

But enough about my daughter. I am writing, of course, to you about Maggie.

I did not want to agree with you about her boyfriend, Tom. I wanted to like him, or at least think he wasn't so bad as to worry about Maggie. And I cannot say, honestly, that I worry about Maggie. She is a tough one, a smart one. Tom seems to rely on that, and perhaps it isn't the healthiest relationship, but I can only imagine Maggie coming out of it even stronger than she is. But I have given myself away here—saying that she will come out of it. Unfortunately, I don't think either you or me will have much influence on when or how, but I do think she'll get out just fine. And I will add that I do hope the sooner the better.

But you should be proud of her. She is beautiful, smart, and a survivor. How many broken hearts have we suffered? Particularly in our youth? And with young people now, it is even more common.

Their new apartment is very near mine here in the former GDR. I am a bit surprised they chose here, but it is cheaper, and I believe it is a very big space.

I tell you all this not knowing if Maggie is in touch with you herself. I gather not, from what you and she tell me. I also tell you everything feeling that I haven't broken her confidence. Nor do I want to be anything but a good sister to you. You may not believe that, but I do.

I say this, and immediately what comes to mind is

my leaving you, when Vati remarried. I know I had no choice, but you didn't know that. You were a child. And even though I had no choice, I still felt horrible about it. But you must know that.

I also want to be someone your daughter can trust. Sometimes I wonder if my love for your daughter is my desire to make it up to you, to repair what I fear I irreparably broke. On the other hand, I worry you think I am trying to come between you and Maggie. And hurt you more.

My intentions are good, and I think I can be a help to you both.

I hope all is well for you. Please write back when you can.

In Liebe,
Deine Eva

CHAPTER 26

It was a Saturday, early in the day for Eva; she had planned to wake up early enough to still have motivation. She had decided to stop by Maggie and Tom's. It had been nearly three weeks since the night out at Café Einstein. She'd spoken to Maggie once on the hall phone. Maggie had said, "I'm off Saturdays. Stop by anytime." Finally, Eva was going to do it. It was past time for a visit.

The day was oddly gorgeous. The gray streets almost seemed bright with sun, the air was sharp, but not painfully so. It was as if spring had come two months earlier than usual. She carried a parcel of chocolates and pastries that she had picked up the night before. She had wanted everything taken care of beforehand. So often, something derailed her. Her weak nerves, her painful legs, her generalized fear, her melancholy. How many days had passed when the only thing she could do was listen to her records and pray? It took all of her energy to prepare for this outing.

And then, parked in front of her building was Hansi in the Cadillac, talking on a phone in his car. It was the most absurd thing she'd ever seen. A phone in a car? She'd seen such things, sometimes, walking down the Ku'damm. Her heart began pounding. Her Hansi was so full of surprises.

She walked up to the car and by pressing a button, Hans rolled down the window on the passenger's side. This startled Eva, and she tripped slightly, falling onto the car. Her face reddened.

"Hans, was machst du hier so früh?"

"Eh? Steig ein."

"Ich muss zu meiner Nichte. Ich kann das nicht schon wieder verschieben."

Eva didn't flinch, even though she wanted to. If she didn't go see Maggie today, she had no idea when she'd get it together to see her.

"Dann bring ich dich hin," Hansi said, opening the door for her.

"Okay! Wunderbar."

It was only a twenty minute walk; Eva didn't need a ride. She feared she'd feel rushed with Hans there. A few months ago, she wouldn't have even mentioned Maggie or any obligation. She would have just gone wherever he wanted to take her, gladly. Imposing her life on him was not her norm. She comforted herself with the fact that at least she was going to Maggie's. And maybe they could set up a date to have lunch or to see each other again soon. It was not a waste, no. Even if it was going to be a brief visit.

Hans drove without asking directions. When Eva gave him the address, he said he knew.

"Wie kommt das? Dass du die Adresse von meiner Nichte kennst?"

He smiled broadly. "I met them both, the day they were visiting you. While you were getting ready, I was downstairs, they came down."

"Yes, but you know where they live?"

"Warum nichts? Tom is an enterprising young man. He won't be fixing the apartment forever."

Eva was shocked. How could they be in contact without her knowing it? It seemed a horrible secret for Maggie to keep from her. She was angry at her niece, and at Hans. But she said nothing. The way he kept stealing glances at her with that smile on his face, she didn't want to give him any more satisfaction. His love of secrets she put up with, but this time it was too much.

Hansi parked the car.

"Kommst du mit?" she asked, as she opened the door to let herself out.

"Warum nicht?"

They walked toward a modern four-story, Soviet-style apartment building—built in the 1960s like Eva's, only smaller—on a corner of a quiet block. On the sidewalk in front of the building next to Maggie and Tom's, dark-skinned children played with a ball. As they neared, Eva saw how unwashed they were, how young they were to be alone on the street. No doubt both of their parents, not to mention uncles and aunts and grandparents, were slaving away at some low-level job for a pittance. The buildings on the other end of the block were boarded up, except for the one at the very end; it was a shell, having been burned down. Arson. So common no one even thought twice to investigate. Another crappy building gone? Good.

There were no buzzers, no names near the front of the door. Eva felt nervous and clutched the bag of pastries tightly. The front door was ajar and, before she could do anything, Hans pushed it open and began walking up the stairs.

It was dark; there was a light in the hallway, but not a bright one. This comforted Eva. Sometimes her building didn't feel well lit, though it was a fine building, fine enough. Sometimes a light in the hallway would be out for weeks before it got changed. So here was a light. That was good sign.

Each floor had two doors. On the second floor, one of the doors lay wide open, revealing an abandoned apartment. On the third floor, Hans stopped and started banging on a closed door that looked newly painted. In fact, Eva could smell the strong, chemical odor of fresh paint. This warmed her more. They cared. They'd been painting.

"*Sie werden noch schlafen, vermute ich,*" Hans said, and Eva looked at him harshly. Then he pounded on the door even more.

"*Es reicht!*" Eva said. The noise embarrassed her, angered her. Although she wasn't sure anyone else lived in the building.

Hans turned to her. She'd angered him, but just then Maggie opened the door, in loose pajamas, her hair tousled, her face without makeup and badly scarred. With makeup her skin had always been rough looking, but without it, Eva now saw, her complexion was even worse.

"Eva! Hans. What are you doing here?" she asked, rubbing her eyes.

"I came to visit. I brought pastries," Eva began, nervously. "I wanted to see you. Perhaps I should have called, but you know how I rarely use the hall phone. And you are so close! I knew you didn't work on Saturdays and when we spoke last you said I could just stop by anytime."

"Come in, come in." Maggie ushered her guests in. "I think it's about time we bought you your own phone, Tante Eva. Come. I'll make some coffee."

The apartment was enormous—they had the whole floor. They must have had a wall knocked down. It was clearly two apartments put together. The smell of paint was strong and the walls were fresh white, blue, and lavender. The far wall, facing the back of the apartment, appeared to be an unfinished mural of some kind. A big mattress lay on the floor near the mural. The sun shone brightly on the white sheets that lay about. They had woken her, that was for sure. She herself often slept this late. She couldn't judge.

"Tom is sleeping in the back room," Maggie said, nodding toward a closed door at the far end of the apartment. "He got in very late last night. So he didn't want to bother me." She said this delicately, as if she were appreciative and yet embarrassed as well.

"Your apartment is lovely, Maggie. And you painted it. It's beautiful, really," Eva said. There wasn't a lot of furniture, but that didn't surprise her. They hadn't been here long. Maggie started making coffee on a portable electric burner.

"We don't have a proper kitchen set up yet. So as you can see, this is how I make coffee. But Tom is very good at that sort of thing. He's working on it."

"*Ja*, and I am helping him get a good price on a stove and a refrigerator," Hans said.

Eva stared at him in wonder. Then she turned to Maggie, who began walking back into the darker part of the flat, carrying a tray with coffees.

"Here, sit down back here. I just need to turn a light on."

There was a small table surrounded by chairs, and Maggie turned on a light hanging from the ceiling. A bare bulb, like the one in the hallway, although this one was bright. Too bright, in fact. Eva felt her face flush. She hated too-strong light. It wasn't flattering.

Maggie sat across from her. She smiled weakly at her aunt, and Eva could see that her eyes were clear. Hans did not sit with them. He walked around the room impatiently, his arms folded behind his back, examining the mural.

"Tom made that," Maggie said. "He's painting again, which is just wonderful. He's always happier and more at ease when he's working on his art."

"How's teaching?"

"It's going well. They've given me some more classes."

Maggie looked down at her coffee. "I'm very busy now. Which is good."

"Are you the only ones in the building?"

"Yes. I mean, no. Well, I'm not sure. There were some people living on the ground floor. But now I'm not sure."

"Are you squatting? Do you have a lease?"

Hans was heading back to where Tom was supposedly sleeping. He opened the door to the room without knocking and shut it behind him.

Maggie smiled awkwardly. Eva asked, "Is it safe here?"

"I feel safe, Tante. Don't worry."

"I wrote your mother a letter. I don't know how in touch you are with her. I told her you had a good job."

Maggie tilted her head. She looked so innocent, her bleached hair wild about her head like a child who'd been outdoor playing. "My mother asked you about me?"

"Of course. She's worried about you. About Tom and you. I told her not to worry. That you were doing well. But I wanted to see for myself. To see you. To see where you live." Eva sighed. "My loyalty is to you, Maggie. But I am not sure all of your mother's concerns are without merit."

"She doesn't like Tom. I wouldn't be here if it weren't for Tom. I could never have done something like this, move to Berlin, get a job . . ."

"But you were here before without him."

Maggie paused. "Yes, that's true. But then, I lived off of my parents."

"And now he lives off of you?" Eva asked quietly. She knew she was treading sensitive ground. She had always appreciated Maggie's forthrightness, her honesty, so perhaps Maggie would appreciate it back. It was something they liked about each other—they could be vulnerable to each other.

"I never think of it that way." Maggie paused and sipped her coffee. "True, I have the job. But he brings in money. He does."

"Do you pay any rent?"

"Two hundred dollars a month. Mostly Tom works on the building—fixes things. It's a great deal."

That was a lot of money to Eva, but she knew it wasn't a lot in general. Not for this space. "And Hans? He got you the apartment?" Eva asked, gulping with emotion. Why was she in this position? How could no one have told her?

"Yeah! So kind of him. He owns the building," Maggie said, yawning. "He didn't tell you?"

Later, Hans and Eva were silent in the car. Eva knew from the direction they were going in that they were heading to Wandlitz. But then he exited, sharply.

"*Wohin fahren wir?*"

"*Was sollen all die Fragen? Eh?*" He hit the steering wheel for emphasis.

"*Ich habe noch mehr!* I have more questions. I do!" Eva choked on her words. He was the only one! The only one she had. She would never have a lover again.

"Frau! Du treibst mich in den Wahnsinn! Wirklich! Es reicht! Es reicht, dage ich! Hast du gehört? Du!?"

Eva looked out the window. The day was ending. The sun's warmth was giving way. They were going to the cabin. She knew it. But she had asked anyway. Tears rolled down her face, and she wiped them quickly. She didn't want them to smear her makeup. She reached in her purse for her pills and managed to shake out a nighttime pill. It would help.

The next morning, waking up in the cool cabin, a blanket of snow leading to the lake, Eva was moved by the quiet beauty. It was deathly, perfectly silent. Of course, her part of the city was quite desolate, but this was a different desolation, the country. It was very early, and yet she was wide awake. Hans lay next to her under the heavy wool blankets, his head propped up on a hard pillow. He was snoring delicately. There had been no more arguing the night before. No more talking really, except for him ordering her to get him a beer, or boil water. No, they had had a quiet evening, a good evening, really. No more had been said, and that was good.

Just now, right before she woke, Eva had dreamed of home, of Leoben. In the dream, her mother looked as she had on her death bed, except she was not thin; she had the robust, womanly body she had before she got sick. She wore one of her dresses, a smart blue flowered dirndl with a yellow apron that she had made herself. She had made dirndls for Liezel and Eva, too. She had been an excellent seamstress, like most Austrian

women from her time. In the dream, Eva stared longingly at
her mother's warm, big body; how she had buried herself in
it so often, as a young girl. But her mother's face was covered
with purple sores, and her skin was greenish and sickly. It was
her deathbed face, but it was also Maggie's face, as Eva realized
on waking. In the dream they were in the kitchen together, Eva
sitting down at the table watching her mother.

"I'm making potato dumpling, Evalein, your favorite!"
she said and smiled at Eva. She was kneading the dough on a
wooden board, then slapping it and shaping it into balls.

"Oh, Mutti, wie wunderbar!" Eva could see herself sitting at
the table, clasping her hands like a young girl. But she was the
woman she was now—dark red hair, the face of middle age,
strong makeup. "But you are dead, Mutti! How can you cook
for me?"

Her mother laughed. "Dead? What does dead mean? I am
here now, cooking, no?"

"Yes," Eva said. "But this is a dream."

"So it is." Her mother said. "And I am dead, and I am cooking for you. You need me. You need someone to take care of
you, Evalein. So I will take care of you. Even though I am dead,
and even though this is just a dream."

It was meant to be a comforting dream. In the dream, Eva
had been comforted. But on waking, it disturbed her to think
of her mother's face like that again. Whenever Eva did think of
her mother, she thought of her as she was before she was sick,
before her face became so disfigured. Now there it was: her

death face, her lovely mother's death face, smiling at her in her dreams.

Eva stood quietly, trying not to wake Hans. This was not easy, as the floorboards in the cabin squeaked. He turned on his side and snorted as she moved, but his breathing stayed shallow. Quietly she wrapped herself in a thick wool coat that he'd left in the cabin and shoved her feet into a pair of rubber boots he kept there as well. She stepped outside and walked toward the lake. Halfway there, she squatted, lifting her skirt with her already cold hands, and relieved herself in the snow. Her urine hissed and the warmth of her fluids melted the snow, mist rising toward her. Using her left hand, as she was taught as a girl, but without the help of a leaf, she wiped herself, her vagina still sore, almost hot, from last night, from Hans's rough, quick time with her. It was okay he was quick. It was cold; quick was good in the cold. She wiped her hand in the snow, then on her coat; then she smelled it. Mossy. Slaty. Then awkwardly standing, grunting to do so, she continued down to the lake. It was a small lake, or a big pond, frozen smooth. On the other side of it was another cabin or an outbuilding of some sort. There was a path through the woods that circled around most of the pond, and Eva took it. She walked quickly, her breath coming out in a wet fog.

The path was littered with the roots of the pines and the smaller trees and shrubs. Occasionally Eva tripped, but she didn't fall. She had to duck her head, too, as the branches came down low. Stooped and tripping, she made it to the other cabin, which on closer inspection was a boathouse. Two large doors stood padlocked in the front, toward the lake, and on the side was a window with no glass. Eva looked in. Two rowboats, one stacked on the other, sat next to a large metal locker. She circled around the house and on the other side saw a large outdoor cellar door, padlocked. She grabbed the door handle and shook it. The skin of her hands cracked in the cold, the metal nearly ripping flesh from her.

"Ach!" she said, frustrated with the lock, with herself, with the secrets she didn't know and wasn't sure she wanted to know. She walked around to the front door and saw that it wasn't properly locked. The cold had burst the hinge out of its sockets and the door was stuck ajar an inch. Despite her painful hands, she grabbed the wooden door and pulled to open it, struggling against the crusty snow but eventually getting it open enough for her to squeeze through. The lockers were well locked, and she didn't want to ruin her hands any more than she already had. She walked up to the boats and sat leaning against them for a while, warming her sore hands between her legs, the coolness feeling almost good on her privates. She closed her eyes. Not for long. She needed the fire.

The way back seemed easier, as always. Her feet had grown so quickly used to the terrain. When she returned, Hans was still sleeping.

CHAPTER 27

Eva had not been her mother's favorite. A firstborn daughter was a disappointment back then. A daughter was for the third or fourth child, so as to have someone to take care of you when you got older. But then Willi was born, and he was the center of her mother's heart. A healthy, noisy, troublesome boy. This is what people wanted then. They wanted sons.

But even if she had not been her mother's favorite, her mother loved her. She was a big warm woman, and she had been very young when she had her children—not yet twenty when Eva was born. Her mother kissed and hugged but was also quick to swat and scold. She was not unique, not special in any way with her kids. But she was good enough. Good enough indeed.

When she got sick, of course, everything changed. Eva was old enough to be strong about it. Any fear and sadness she kept so well hidden she didn't even remember feeling it, not even after her mother died. It was as if laundry and shopping for cheap meals and sewing the clothes and keeping the floors clean became her emotional life. And taking care of Liezel.

Liezel was all hers then. And she loved that. That was how she remembered it. The house, particularly getting meals together was sometimes stressful and overwhelming. But Liezel was her prize.

Not that it had been so easy, winning Liezel away from her mother. But it hadn't been so hard, either. As her mother became more sick and spent more time in the hospital, Liezel seemed to forget her. That's how children are. They move on, so quickly it can take your breath away. They're built for survival.

The older we get, thought Eva, the more we sabotage ourselves, our survival. The more all those things we handled so bravely as children come back to haunt us, tear us apart, render us frozen and useless.

Eva was awake but not out of bed. It was noon. She'd come back late the night before, after spending two quiet and uneventful days with Hans at the cabin. Strangely for her, she was happy when he dropped her off last night, happy to be away from him, and she had stayed up late listening to music.

A banging on the door startled her. "Eva," Krista said. "Eva, the phone is for you."

She wrapped her robe around her and went out.

"I'm sorry if I woke you," Krista said, with a slight, weird smile on her lips. "I thought you would want to be woken for a phone call."

"Yes, of course. I was awake. Just not up yet. Thank you for getting me."

Krista smiled even more nervously, looking at her feet.

"*Ja bitte?*" Eva said into the phone.

"Eva? It's Liezel. I'm so happy I caught you."

"Liezel!"

"I'm coming to Berlin."

Eva's heart started to beat rapidly. She hadn't had her coffee yet. It was all too much.

"I won't stay long. But I may try and bring back Maggie. I know I can't force her back, but I'm worried. You see, she called and asked for money. It appears Tom has gotten himself arrested."

Eva felt the heat run to her face. How did Liezel know this and not her?

"Arrested? For what? Is Maggie okay?" She had a sudden feeling of anger at Maggie, for not calling her first, for not letting her know. Eva went back to her room to get a pen and paper to write down Liezel's hotel info. Her room, her haven, glared at her cheaply; she did not want her sister to see how she lived.

"She didn't tell me why Tom was arrested, just that he was. And that she needed money to get him out of jail. If I ask her questions, she doesn't answer. That's how it is with her. She thinks her life is none of my business."

"I wrote you and told you that I agreed that perhaps Tom wasn't the best . . ."

Liezel interrupted, "I know. I got the letter already. I appreciated it."

"But I still am shocked about this."

"I'm not," Liezel said, grimly. "How often are you seeing Maggie? I mean, are you even looking out for her?"

Eva felt that blackness pour through her. She was supposed to take care of Liezel, now Maggie, and nothing she did was ever enough. And who takes care of her? Who ever took care of her? Her rich younger sister? Her dead mother? Her selfish dead husband? "Of course I'm looking out for her, but she's not an infant whose diapers I can change like yours."

"What is that supposed to mean?"

"She came here because she loves it here and not there, and I don't blame her."

"She doesn't know what she loves. She's a child. Jesus, Eva."

The images of Liezel a bit younger than Maggie, the photos that Elena made her look at, came at her, her youth and beauty used as a weapon, her betrayal of her only sister, of the only person alive *who loved her. Who truly loved her.*

"Anyway, Eva, I'm coming to get her."

"You knew she was a drug addict and so was her boyfriend and you let her leave? To move to Berlin?" Eva asked and closed her eyes, letting her head fall back. "I haven't failed you. You failed *her.*"

"She bought the ticket without telling me! She did everything without telling me until after she did it! What was I supposed to do?" Liezel was yelling now.

It was as if Eva woke up. "I'll go by there today."

"I think she's at work." Liezel was breathing heavily.

"I'll go by later, when she's off of work. She doesn't live far from me."

"I know," Liezel said. And now the crying. The sniffling. "She doesn't love me, my daughter, but you know that already." Eva then heard her take a deep breath. "I do think she needs me right now. I think she's been humbled."

Eva was at a loss. *"Es tut mir leid."* The anger hadn't gone, but it was washed over with shame. Remorse.

"Mir auch," Liezel said, but Eva detected a flatness in her tone. She had never shown remorse for anything. It was if when Eva left her, when she was abandoned, something in her shut down toward Eva. And yet, here she was. And here was her daughter.

"I'm going to the airport now," Liezel said. "I'm just getting on the next plane to Berlin. See you soon. How long has it been?"

"A long time."

"No need to pick me up at the airport. I'll call you when I get to the hotel."

"Wunderbar."

Eva put her hands to her face after she hung up. Her face was hot, and she couldn't see well out of her left eye. She went back to her room and lay down and tried to breathe slowly.

Krista knocked again. "Eva," she said outside the closed door, *"Ist alles okay?"*

"Ja, ich habe Kopfschmerzen, nichts weiter," Eva said loudly, shrilly, leaning her head toward the door. She hated that, talking

through the thin doors. It was so uncivilized. She always stood up and opened it. But not today. She wanted Krista to go away. *"Ich kann jetzt nicht mit dir sprechen."*

When evening came, Eva put on a record that she had bought a long time ago from an unknown blues singer from the East— not a Black person but a Romanian man named Alexei Bondy, singing in English. He sang in a very heavily accented English, and the album was very scratched up. She had listened to it a lot when Hugo had been alive. When she would listen to anything bluesy. It had been a long time. It was beautiful. What did it matter, who sang the blues? She rouged and powdered her face, and he sang about making peace with where he was, with a knife in hand and blood on the wall.

She lifted the needle from the record when the song was finished. Carefully, she put the album away.

CHAPTER 28

She wore her good walking shoes, black lace-ups she'd bought fifteen years ago. They weren't pretty, but she didn't care. She had always taken good care of them, twice a year taking them to the cobbler to maintain them. He was gone now, the cobbler; everything was gone now.

As she walked, she noticed the skinheads were out on their corner for the first time in quite a while. She began to walk more quickly, with determination. She wasn't afraid of them; she was not afraid of anything right now, but she was angry that they were there. They were a stain on her city. A disgrace. As she approached the three men, she noticed that they looked awful. Thinner, their complexions greener and more mottled. One of them, the smallest of the three, shivered uncontrollably even though he wore a black leather jacket and a hat.

The little one came toward her and she veered away into the street, but he kept coming. Eva kept walking. She did not run, but then, for some reason, she felt compelled to look back at him. *"Fräulein,"* he said. *"Können Sie mir helfen? Ich sterbe wahrscheinlich bald."*

Eva stopped. He was shivering so much, he could barely stand, bent over, drooling. *"Was? Drogen töten immer. Das muss dir doch klar sein, Junge?"* she snapped. Why was she talking to this cruel, horrible boy?

"Meine Mutter will nicht mit mir sprechen. Aber hier, hier ist ihre Nummer." He tried to hold out a piece of paper with a name and phone number on it to her, but he dropped it. Eva quickly picked it up. *"Bitte, Fräulein. Ich kann sehen, dass Sie eine gute Frau sind."*

Eva said nothing. He had turned away, walking back to his friends. She kept going toward Maggie's. What had happened to them? Such a sudden change. She shoved the paper into her pocket. As she got close to Maggie's, she saw a Turkish restaurant on the corner. She decided to go in and have a coffee, maybe a brandy. Inside, there was one table occupied by three Turkish men, smoking, talking in Arabic. They stopped talking when she came in, looking at her. Two other small tables were empty and she sat at the nearest one. One of the men came to her.

"Einen Kaffee und einen Brandy, bitte."

The man said nothing but shortly brought her a sweet, Turkish coffee and a small glass of brandy. She drank the brandy first. It was sharp and cheap but she didn't care. She took out the piece of paper the skinhead had given her, sipping the thick, cloying coffee. Frau Baerbel Weber. The number was local. She carefully folded the paper and put it in her wallet. And if she were to call this woman? It would be what

Jesus would have done. Loving thine enemies. The sweetness of the coffee clung, but grounds at the the gritty bottom of the pretty, tiny cup, stuck like mud to her tongue. She could see the darkness of it in her mouth, in her mind, she saw it.

One thing at a time. She dropped some money and left without saying anything, which felt unlike her, was unlike her.

In the twenty minutes it took Eva to walk to Maggie's apartment, the evening turned to night. Eva never walked around this part of Berlin at night if she could help it. She had left the house later than she thought. Standing outside of Maggie's building, waiting for the wave of fear, of apprehension to rise inside of her, Eva fumbled around in her purse, looking for her nighttime pills, but her heart beat only slightly faster than normal—she had been walking quickly, after all—and her mind did not jump around with terrible thoughts. She stopped searching for her pills and closed her eyes. *Jesus, bist du bei mir?* She pushed at the door—it was open. The calmness she felt was so unlike her normal state of mind. She didn't trust it, but she tried to. *Danke, Jesus. behütest du mich?* God was giving her strength. It was the only explanation. When she reached Maggie's apartment, she knocked firmly. No one answered. She knocked again, banging hard this time. A door on the ground floor opened and a middle-aged Turkish woman came to the hall and looked up the stairs.

"*Das Mädchen ist drinnen,*" she said, in heavily accented German. "*Ich habe sie gesehen.*"

"*Danke,*" Eva replied. She tried the doorknob and the door swung open easily. It had been unlocked. Hot rage knifed through Eva. How could Maggie be so careless? Maggie the teacher, Maggie, her American niece who loved her? How could she be so stupid?

Quickly the rage dissipated and she saw the shadow of her niece on a large floor pillow by the back windows. It was dark in the apartment. The calmness that infected Eva earlier came back. Maggie is dead, she thought. And it's not my fault. But she saw her niece stir, ever so slightly.

"Tom? Tom?" Maggie lifted her head slightly.

"No, Maggie. It's Eva."

"Oh no."

"Oh no?" Eva shut the door behind her and reached around the walls, looking for a light switch. She gave up and walked to Maggie, her eyes slowly adjusting. "Why 'oh no,' Maggie? It's me. It's just me."

"I don't want you seeing me like this." Maggie's voice was hoarse. "I'm ashamed."

Eva sat next to her. The apartment smelled bad, like sour fruit, the fresh smell of paint gone. Eva wanted to ask where a light was. She wanted to turn on the lights. But it didn't seem the right thing to do.

"Your mother is coming." She reached out to her niece, to stroke her hair. It was damp with sweat and thick with dirt. "Why did you call your mother? Why didn't you call me first? I am here for you. Me. I am here."

"I know," she sighed. "But I can't borrow money from you, can I?"

So this is what it came down to. It wasn't trust or the lack of it. How could Eva help her when she had nothing to give? "I could have asked Hans. He has money."

"I could have asked Hans," Maggie said, drily. "But that would have been too ironic."

"What does that mean? And what about Elena? After all she did for you?" Eva couldn't contain her anger now. "She would have helped you."

"I've asked enough of Elena," Maggie said. "Also, she wasn't crazy about Tom. The money is for him."

"Who is crazy about Tom," said Eva. It wasn't a question. "No one is." Then, "Maggie, what happened to you? What is wrong? Why has everything gone so wrong?"

Maggie sat up, groaning. Even in the dark, Eva could tell Maggie was a mess. A complete mess. Not like before. Not secretly a mess. Something had changed. Eva was furious, but she tried to hide it.

"I'm sorry, Tante Eva. I know I've disappointed you."

Eva stopped touching Maggie's hair and then touched her stomach, then her face, then lifted her arms. She was a nurse, after all. Her stomach was hard—not a good sign, a blockage? Her face was cold; her arms had marks, needle marks.

"We need to get you to a hospital."

"That might be the right thing to do."

"Yes. I'll walk you there."

"I don't think I can walk very far." Maggie began to cry.

"Of course. We'll call a taxi."

"I have no phone. It got shut off. We didn't pay the bill. Actually, that was the one bill Tom was supposed to take care of. He didn't pay it. The one thing I have him do, and he doesn't do it."

"I'll go downstairs. The woman who lives there may have a phone."

"Maybe," said Maggie. "I don't know."

Eva pulled Maggie to her, embracing her horrible body. "What happened, Maggie? What happened?"

"I use heroin, Tante Eva. Please don't hate me. And lately, I've been shooting bad drugs. Really bad drugs. Things just got worse, too. I don't know."

"I'm going downstairs to call a car. I'll be right back. You'll be fine. Don't worry," Eva said, realizing how stupid she sounded. But what was she supposed to say? Her anger at her niece left her. She was in need of help. Who didn't need help? What human being doesn't make mistakes, doesn't need someone to hold them up?

"You know, Tante Eva, that Tom beat up a whore? That's why he's in jail. He almost killed her. A fucking whore. How hard is it to get arrested for that? And he's been dealing heroin for Hans. Hans's drugs are bad, though. They're cut with something awful, and that's what's been making me sick. I'm so mad. I'm not even mad at him. I don't care about him. I'm so mad at myself," she said, her voice thick with snot and tears.

"Hans?"

"We assumed you knew. I mean, he's your boyfriend."

"Yes, he's my boyfriend. But he's no drug dealer," Eva spat. Then she thought of the cabin, of the boxes, of the late night at the gas station. Maggie was smiling through her obvious pain, her physical discomfort.

"Come on, Tante Eva. You have to be kidding me! What doesn't Hans deal?"

"What a thing to say." Eva closed her arms over her chest. "And leave Tom to rot in jail."

"I'm sorry. I'm sorry." Maggie bent over, her arms wrapping around her waist. "Please don't be angry at me. You're the only one I have. You're the only person I can trust."

"How is it you've held down your job in this condition?"

"I've called in sick once. But I manage."

Eva looked at her hard; she looked like death. "I find that hard to imagine."

"My job means a lot to me. It's my freedom from my parents. It's not like I'm running a company. Or even being a nurse, like you were. I'm just trying to teach English to some desperate immigrants. As long as I show up and hand out some worksheets, it's all fine."

"That's terrible, Maggie. I thought you would care more, care more about the people you teach. They need to learn German to make it in this country."

"I do care. And most of the time I've been a good teacher. All I'm saying is, on a bad day, I still show up and manage, that's all. Please don't be angry at me." But it was true, the feelings of disappointment and shock kept coming back to Eva. The worst was when her thoughts returned to herself. How could Maggie do this to me? thought Eva. Immediately, she was ashamed. Maggie didn't do anything to Eva. She did this to herself. Not that it didn't affect everyone around her, but still, it wasn't about them. It was about Maggie.

"We are going to get you to a hospital." And then she thought of what she didn't want to think. How the mind works, how it goes to where it goes, regardless of our hearts' desires. Hans and his mysterious packages near the Polish border. Hans. Her Hansi. Her everything.

"How could I have loved him?" Maggie bawled. "How could I have loved someone so awful?"

Eva felt a calmness again. Like the calmness she felt on coming here. *Bitte, mein Gott. Bitte hilf uns.* "You're not to blame for having loved anyone. All you did was love. It is not a crime, not even to love someone awful. People think love can change others. Sometimes, we love awfulness thinking we can love it away. This isn't a bad thing."

In the cab, Maggie said, "I can't do it."

"Yes you can. I'll help you. Your mother will help you. There's medication they can give you, too. To make it less painful," Eva said.

"My mother help me? Seeing my mother will make me want to shoot up ten times more than usual." Maggie looked away from Eva, out the window of the cab. "I know a place that has good drugs. Different drugs. Better ones. If I can get some good stuff in me, then I'll get clean." Maggie grabbed Eva's arm. "I'm going to do drugs today no matter what. It's not your fault. It's mine. But nothing you do can save me from myself."

Maggie began scratching herself all over. Her eyes bulged and she said very quietly, "Heroin is my love, my one true love. Not Tom. Not my family, even. No one can tell me what not to love. Didn't you say that to me, Tante Eva?"

What could Eva say? Eva fumbled in her purse for a sleeping pill, just one, to calm her nerves. She quickly swallowed it, without any water, dry and chalky in her throat. She wanted to say, Then why did you call her and not me? Why did you call *her*? "You tell the cab where to go, if that's what you need to do."

Twenty minutes later, Eva found herself in Kreuzberg, outside a building not unlike the one Maggie and Tom lived in, just busier, drug addicts coming and going. She waited in the cab while her niece bought drugs. She's an ingrate, thought Eva. My niece, who thinks so much of me, who has some of the socialist spirit, is really a spoiled and ungrateful child, thought Eva, as she watched the sad, stumbling people come and go, the door always opening and closing, opening and closing.

CHAPTER 29

It had been nearly three decades, or longer—Eva's mind began to hum with panic that she wasn't quite sure; how was it she wasn't sure?—since she'd seen Liezel. Now, in this fancy hotel lobby on the Ku'damm, Eva waited nervously. It was far earlier than she usually woke, never mind actually being somewhere. She was so anxious she almost didn't feel tired. The receptionist had called up to Liezel's room; she was coming down. Eva wore the red dress and had carefully applied lipstick. But she was sweating from nerves, and she felt she could smell herself. Maybe she'd put on too much cologne, but at least it might cover up her smell, the smell of fear.

Why fear? On the one hand, it seemed natural. It had been so long, it was just a big moment. But on the other hand, it seemed wrong. This was her sister. Her sister. Eva began humming to herself that Billie Holiday song she liked, "Long Gone Blues."

"Talking to yourself!" Liezel was there suddenly.

Eva stood. There she was, immediately with the criticism,

pretending it was all in good fun. They hugged, and then it was all so sudden, the feel of her body, how it was the same body and yet different, very much older. The hug was tight but trembly. It was awkwardly long. Eva wasn't sure when to let go, so she decided to wait for Liezel to. Finally, they looked, really looked, at each other. Liezel was middle-aged. Her eyes were the same brown doe eyes, but so much harder. How could this happen? Eva patted her own hair, all the nerves in her body lit.

"I was humming a song. From a record Maggie gave me." Eva began laughing nervously. She covered her mouth, self conscious of her nervousness, the feeding cycle of it all. She was nervous, then ashamed of being nervous, which made her do things that made her feel more nervous. Her sister was still beautiful, but her mouth had deep creases and her hair was gray. Eva wondered why she didn't color it. That seemed odd, to not color your gray hair. Especially in America, where coloring your hair must be easy, like everything else. Like buying food, and driving a car, and having a big house.

Liezel was wearing a soft cotton blouse and thin wool trousers, both in subdued grays. Eva immediately felt loud. Her dress was loud. She'd done it again, thought things through the wrong way. She thought the dress would make her feel glamorous. But it was her sister who was glamorous, in her subtle, fine fabrics.

"Let's have a coffee, Eva. You look great. I love your dress."

She followed her sister into the dining room at the hotel. The tables were set with white linen, and waiters in vests and bow ties walked around. Eva couldn't help but be excited to sit here, in this lovely place. She had brought some money, but she was hoping Liezel would pay.

The menu was small and very expensive. Even more expensive than Café Einstein.

"I feel I should ask all about you, but I really want to talk about Maggie," Liezel said.

"You don't need to ask all about me," said Eva. "My life is very simple. So there wouldn't be so much to say. Talk to me about Maggie."

"She claims she won't come back. Maybe you could help me convince her otherwise. She immediately has to disagree with anything I say. She has to make it look like she doesn't need me. And believe me, I wish she didn't. I had a child at her age. What is it with young people these days? It's as if they stay teenagers their whole lives."

"She's a good girl, too. She's not all bad."

"She's a drug addict."

"Yes, but she'll leave Tom, I think. I don't think she'll be taking him back." Eva immediately thought of Hans and then banished the thought. She looked around the beautiful room. Mozart played gently in the background. Liezel stared at her.

"You knew." Her sister's face burned slightly. Anger, thought Eva. How it makes us glow. Like when we make love.

"You knew, Liezel. I want to help with Maggie. I want to help Maggie and help you. At first, I just had my suspicions and they weren't strong enough to risk saying something that could or could not be true."

"Okay," Liezel said. "I'm sorry. I'm just so frustrated."

Eva looked at her baby sister and saw her for what she was; an angry, desperate woman in middle age. Dry-skinned, jowly with worry, a life that hadn't turned out as it should've. A mentally ill husband. A drug-addicted, child-ish grown daughter. But whose life does become the life of their dreams? Then, fleetingly, Eva saw her as a little three-year-old, laughing and hugging her. And then, as the young woman she became—that combination of innocence and sexuality that is irresistible to most men, and many women, too. It is not just time that changes people. *We go away. We become wholly different.*

"I understand," Eva said. Was she responsible? Because of Hansi? Now her face burned red, too. "I think I'll order a schnapps."

"This early?"

"Yes, this early. It's very good for the digestion."

Liezel looked at her watch.

"I need her address. Maybe even you can take me to her house?"

"I'll give you her address. I don't think I should go there with you."

"Why? I need you!" Eva didn't want a scene, but Liezel

seemed not to care. She was being loud. "You know she likes you better than me." Tears welled in her eyes. "And I'm scared of your neighborhood. It's a ghetto." Then, gathering herself, she said, "You're used to it. I don't want to go alone."

Liezel, needing her. Rich, American Liezel. Pretty Liezel, what had she ever done for her? Besides fuck her husband? Coolly, she took out a small notebook from her purse and wrote down the address. "Here," she said. "You'll be fine if you take a cab. Have the driver wait until you are in the building."

"What if she doesn't want to go home with me?" Liezel asked.

Eva saw in her mind the dark hallway of the building she'd taken Maggie to so she could buy drugs, smelled the wet burning smell it omitted, a smell she could smell even from the cab.

Liezel continued. "I already know she doesn't want to come back with me. But it doesn't matter what she wants anymore. What is she going to do? Stay here and die? Have you look after her?" Liezel let out a short, mean laugh. Then she leaned across the table. "I'll win. I've won. I was right, all along," she said, shaking her head. "Children. They think they know everything. They're all so stupid." Liezel stared sharply at her, straight at Eva, taking a sip of her coffee.

Eva looked away from her sister. Hatred, that oily blackness—hatred was what Eva felt for this woman, this person her sister had become. She hated her for getting old and pathetic. For wielding her little bit of power so shamelessly. Eva sat back, holding her tiny schnapps glass. She downed it. And what did her sister think of her? Even less than what she thought of Liezel?

"I have a daughter too, you know." She looked back at her sister. "You'd be surprised how quickly everything changes. Someday, you'll need Maggie. You might want to consider that."

Liezel leaned back. Eva could see her breathing heavily. "I think I'll first worry about my daughter," Liezel said. "Then she can worry about me when the time comes."

And then it was as if Eva felt nothing. "I need you to pay me back for all the money I've been spending on taking care of Maggie. I took her on cab rides when she wasn't well."

"Cab rides?"

"Yes, it was then that I became suspicious something was wrong," Eva lied. "Because normally she could take the U-Bahn."

"How much?" Liezel asked.

"Two hundred marks."

The two sisters looked at each other.

"Konnen wir zahlen, bitte," Liezel asked the waiter as he walked by. She reached in her expensive, large bag with some logo on it that Eva didn't recognize, and took two hundred marks out of her wallet. She put the bills down in front of Eva, and Eva took them.

"You have Elena's number and mine," Eva said. "Call me at either of those places and let me know how it goes. If you need us, we will do what we can."

"I tried calling Maggie, " Liezel said, as they both stood. "The phone was disconnected."

"Tom didn't pay the bill as he was supposed to," Eva said. *"Bis später, Schwester."*

CHAPTER 30

After she returned home on the U-Bahn, Eva sat at her table, thinking, trying to quiet her breath. She drank a brandy, then she left, straight back to the U-Bahn, this time straight to Elena's.

She had a key to Elena's apartment—just in case, an emergency backup key. Elena had one of Eva's as well. Neither had ever used her key to open the other's door. This time, Eva let herself in, turned on the hallway light, went into the living room, and immediately went to the shelves holding endless boxes of film and thick stacks of photo albums, all meticulously labeled. Her daughter often acted and appeared as a sloven, dissolute a bum—goodness, she begged on the U-Bahn for laughs—but she was actually a very organized person—a hard-working, dedicated craftsperson, a brilliant student of the arts. A talented, ambitious artist.

And so without much effort she found the photo album, and she took it out, dust free—Elena dusted all the time, kept everything so clean—and sat on one of the low cushions next to the low, round table with ashtrays and matches. She pulled out all of the photos of Liezel. Holding them was breathtaking. They stole her breath. They were of a lost time, a time of such beauty, of such horror and pain. Carefully, barely shaking, she lit a match and burned one, holding it up to the flame over an ashtray full of cigarette butts. It caught easily and turned purple, to orange with licks of yellow, then back to purple and disintegrated into ash. Ashes to ashes, Eva thought, with great satisfaction. She took another photo of Liezel and then she heard the door open. She hadn't locked it behind her.

Elena came in, in her jeans, throwing her coat off, braless in a sweatshirt. *"Mutti? Was ist hier los? Was zu Teufel! Was machst du da!? Stopp! Stopp, Mutti!"* She ran to her mother, but Eva had already lit another photo, her mouth set. Justice. Justice, not revenge. Sometimes one seems like the other. Sometimes they are the same.

Elena lunged for the photo album, but Eva dropped the burning, ruined photo in the ashtray and grabbed the album and stood, holding it to her chest.

Elena sat, her head in her hands, and wept. *"Mutti, Mutti. Das ist alles, was ich von Vati habe."* She looked up at her mother. *"How can you?"* she screamed and threw herself at her mother. They struggled over the book. Eva held it fast, even after Elena knocked her down. Then Elena grabbed the book, and it ripped in half. Elena sat again, weeping.

"Du," Eva said to her daughter, *"du hast so viel von deinem Vati. Diese Fotos brauchst du nicht."*

She left then, with half the photo album in her arms and her daughter weeping on the floor.

On the train back to her apartment, she clutched the album to her chest as one phrase from the burial prayer ran through her mind over and over again: earth to earth, ashes to ashes, dust to dust.

When she got out, it was dark and the air was so dry, it was like it wasn't even there. She walked toward her apartment without a thought in her head. At the corner were two of the skinheads. The little one wasn't there—the baby skinhead, and she laughed for a quick beat at her thought. Then she remembered the number she carried in her wallet. The two looked so sick, sick like Maggie, sicker than that. One was coatless.

She walked up to them and said to the coatless one, *"Wo ist deine Lederjacke?"*

He looked up, his face blue. He probably had hypothermia. She should call an ambulance.

He said, *"Die hab ich verkauft."* Then, *"Bitte, Fräulein, haben Sie ein bisschen Geld fur uns?"* The other one looked up at her now, his face covered in snot.

"Ich habe kein Geld," she said. *"Aber hier, nimm das."* Then she opened the album. She flipped through the book, and with God's help quickly found the photo she wanted, the one in which Liezel clearly was in ecstasy on top of Hugo. She took it, then handed the book over to the boy, his arms outstretched to receive it.

CHAPTER 31

Back in her apartment, Eva put on the Nina Simone. She poured herself a tall brandy; she hadn't had any lunch. She'd been too embarrassed to eat in front of Liezel, and she didn't eat anything after leaving, either. It burned her stomach, the brandy, but she was hoping it would calm her nerves. After another tall brandy, her stomach no longer burned, but her hands still shook, her teeth were gritted tightly, and her mind was wild with thoughts. Prayer? She took four sleeping pills and tried to pray.

She woke later in her chair. The apartment was dark; it was early morning now. There she sat where she'd been drinking, an open bottle of pills on the table in front of her. Her head throbbed so hard it scared her. And her legs. They felt on fire. After turning on the table lamp she took off her dress and stockings and her left leg in particular burned and went numb. She looked down at it; it was red and mottled, swollen at the joints.

A loud knock on her door startled her. She grabbed for her robe. *"Moment! Moment!"* She hobbled to the door, wiping at

the dried drool glued to her cheek as she opened it. It was
Krista's mother. Eva nearly fell—she couldn't feel her leg—but
she managed to lean against the door, catching herself.

"*Frau Haufmann, wie geht es Ihnen?*" Eva asked.

"*Ich habe Krista seit zwei Tagen nicht mehr gesehen.*" She was
shaking. She gave off a terrible odor. Her head was dirtier than
ever; her clothes, soiled. It must have taken a huge effort to
leave the apartment.

"*Kommen sie herein. Wir besprechen das jetzt und rufen dann
vielleicht die Polizei.*"

"*Die Polizei? Die Polizei?*"

Eva looked at the clock. It was almost 6:00 A.M. She wondered if they should wait an hour or so, in case Krista would
return. But her mother said Krista had never spent the night
away before. Only once or twice with a school friend, but it
was all planned beforehand, and that had been years ago now,
anyway. No, something was wrong. There was no need to wait
longer. Calling the police was something that invoked fear
in Eva as well, not just Mrs. Haufmann. Before the Wall was
down, one would never call the police about anything. Ever.
They were always there, lurking. Everyone was the police, the
regular police or the Stasi. No one called them, too, because
there had never been any crime to speak of. When people went
missing, well, that was different. That was usually at the hands
of the police. It was a different world now.

After calling from the hall phone, Eva waited in Mrs.
Haufmann's apartment with her; it took over two hours for

the police to arrive. They had wanted them to come to the station, but Eva explained Gabi's condition, and they reluctantly agreed to send officers to the apartment. Krista had been acting so strangely, Mrs. Haufmann explained. She was always sick, she was always throwing up, and she had behaved unkindly to her, to her very own mother. She had never prayed during socialism; she knew the futility of it, but she had taken to praying in the past few weeks, because everything seemed so wrong. She remembered prayers from her childhood. What could have happened? Where was her daughter? She asked Eva to call Maggie, to call her daughter, Elena.

"*Frau Haufmann, es besteht nicht die geringste Wahrscheinlichkeit, dass Krista bei Maggie ist.*"

"*Warum sagen Sie das? Wie können Sie das wissen? Ich weiss, dass die beiden befreundet waren. Ich weiß es!*"

Eva's heart sank. She remembered the night at Cafe Einstein. She remembered Tom. She remembered his foot under the table, looking for Krista's. So back to the hallway she went. She called Elena.

"*Mutti! Wie geht's?*"

"*Hast du die Krista gesehen? Oder weißt du, ob sie bei Maggie ist oder war in den letzten beiden Tagen?*"

"*Krista? Deine Nachbarin?*"

"*Genau.*"

"I have no idea where she is, Mutti."

Then Eva remembered the number in her purse. She went back to her apartment and opened her wallet, unfolded the piece of paper. The handwriting was from a woman, not from the skinhead, not from that boy. Frau Weber. She dialed the number.

"*Ja bitte?*" a woman said.

"*Kann ich bitte Frau Weber sprechen?*"

"*Ich bin Frau Weber.*"

"*Frau Weber, Ihr Sohn hat mir Ihre Nummer gegeben.*"

"My son? What? Who are you? My son is dead! *Tot! Tot! Mein Sohn ist tot!*" She started weeping loudly, then screaming, "*Tot, tot!*"

Eva hung up. Of course he's dead. And probably, thought Eva, so was Krista.

She went back to Frau Haufmann's. She explained to her and the police that no one knew where Krista was. No one she knew had seen her.

Eva went back into her apartment. She hadn't mentioned the skinheads. This was her first sin. She turned on the lights and saw everything—her bed, her record player, her little table. It held her warmly for one second, but then anguish set in. Her heart was beating so hard. Her leg! She sat down at her table, and for a moment, she thought she might die of a stroke. She closed her eyes. She thought of Mrs. Haufmann praying. She began to pray. Dear Father, our Father, who art in heaven, hallowed be thy name. She did not call Maggie. Not after where she left her, not after everything. She lied about that. That was her second sin.

. . .

Eva got into bed and immediately fell asleep. When she awoke, she woke slowly, still lost in a dream. In the dream, Hugo was a man in his forties, the man she fell in love with. He was laughing with his friends—they were all there, Wolf, too—and they were sitting in the backyard of their old house. The trees were green; it was summer. The sun shone, and in the dream Eva's arms were slick with warm summer sweat. Her whole life was ahead of her. Of course they'd made mistakes, but there was no end in sight, no end to the possibility that all could be good again. That life would go on and on. In the dream, Elena walks up to Eva, but it is the Elena of now, not Elena the little girl. In the dream, Eva stops her light laughter, the feeling of ease goes away. Then Eva woke up.

She looked at the clock. It was almost 2:00 P.M. She got up, unstable, holding the sides of the wall, but made it to the kitchen to make coffee. She took a morning pill as she waited for the coffee to brew.

The police had been different from the police of the GDR. This was nothing new—a change, a difference, and yet it still felt similar. She didn't like them. She didn't trust them. But they had taken all the information about Krista. They also called for an ambulance and took Mrs. Haufmann away. The fear in her face! The fear in her blind, sickly face. And yet she didn't protest at being taken away. How could she? She couldn't take care of herself.

Eva put on the Billie Holiday record, but it irritated her, so she took it off right away. It was silence she needed. To think. She closed her eyes, sitting at her little table. The coffee began to work on her. She should call Liezel, but she wouldn't. Then, she should go over to Maggie's. She should ask Maggie if she knew where Krista was. The lies, they kept building. They built a small, hard wall inside her.

As she stood to bathe, Hansi knocked on her door. He called to her, "Eva! *Bist du herein?*"

"*Ja! Ja!*" Eva opened the door and there he was. The man who loved her.

"*Komm! Gehen Wir!*"

"*Nein, Ich muss ein shower nehmen.*"

"*Ach! I kann nicht warten!*"

"*Okay, moment, moment.*" So no shower then, she thought, grimly. He waited outside while she got dressed, put on lipstick, sprayed her hair.

Once in the car, her legs began to hurt. She rubbed them.

"*Was is los?*"

"*Meine beine tut mir weh.*"

Hansi grunted. Eva looked at his big, Slavic face. His broad nose, his thick forehead and hair. She smelled him, that wonderful, familiar smell; the cologne, the stale smoke, the oil of his skin.

"My neighbor Krista is missing. The young girl. And her mother, so sick, she can't see, really, she's lost nearly all of her sight—she was taken away too."

Hans said nothing.

"Did you know? Do you know what happened to her?"

"Ich weiss nichts. Ich kenne ihnen nichts."

"Doch. You know them. You've seen Krista over the years."

"Ja, ja. But I don't know them, really. Why do you ask me these questions?"

"Well, you are full of surprises. You know all sorts of things that surprise me. You know where the Stasi kept samples of my smell."

"That's because I was Stasi, Schatzi." Hansi turned to her. *"Aber du weisst dass shon."*

Yes, she knew. But was this something they had ever talked about? No. She knew all sorts of things that she didn't like to think about. Why bother? What could she do? And there was maybe knowing something and then there was really knowing something for certain. There was her faith in God, a belief she kept with her every day, but did she know? Did she have evidence? Her sort of evidence, yes. But the day in and day out of life, these were the things that struck her as even more unknowable than God in heaven who sent a Son to Earth to save their souls. So what did she really know? The world was beyond her.

"Can you take me to Maggie's quickly?"

"I have no time! I have to meet someone."

"Are we going to the cabin?"

"Yes." He looked at her, then back at the road. Just a glance. A glance, and a smile. These things were her heart, her solace.

"Please, I won't stay for long. It's very important. Then we'll go straight to the cabin."

"No."

"I ask so little from you. Why take me on a trip if you can't be bothered to give me ten minutes of time? Maybe I'll get out." They were approaching a red light. Eva unlocked the door and began to open it.

"You're crazy. Stop that." Hans grabbed for her, but he was too big, too cumbersome.

"I'm not crazy. I need to talk with my niece. So I will get out now, if you don't take me." She was stunned when the words came out of her mouth.

Hans looked at her. *"Was? Was hast du mire gesacht?"*

"Bitte, Hansi. I muss meine nichte suchen. Wirklich."

Unbelievably, his face softened. She never spoke like this to him. Or when she did, she always regretted it. But he said, "Okay. Okay. She might be working, you know."

"I want to see if she's there. I will be quick. She doesn't work every day. I forget her schedule. Just wait for me."

"Fine. Shut the door."

They drove to Maggie's in silence. Eva got out and didn't look back. She went up the stairs and knocked tentatively, but the door was open and she went in.

Maggie was there, as well as two other people, a young woman and a young man whom she'd never seen before. They were surrounded by lit candles, and the curtains were pulled. The day was dark, but in the apartment, it was darker.

They were high. There was a faint odor of burning and vomit. Eva straightened her skirt out and put her hand to her heart.

"Tante Eva!" Maggie said. She stood up and then sat back down on the ground, pillows scattered around her on a filthy rug. Here she was, a girl who'd been given everything. Clothes, warmth, a nice house, education—everything anyone could ever ask for. Even a mother's love; whatever Eva thought of her sister, she loved Maggie as well as she could. All the things neither Liezel or she had had, or not for long. And she'd taken everything she was given and thrown it away. Eva closed her eyes and saw the rooms of her life, her childhood room that she shared with Willi and Liezel, her house with Hugo, the room she lived in now. You think everything is forever, but it all goes away. Maggie probably thought she could always go home, but someday, her home would be gone.

"Your mother came looking for you, Maggie."

"I should be angry at you, Tante Eva," Maggie said, smoking a cigarette.

"Angry at me?"

"You gave that witch my address."

"You called her. She came here because of you."

Maggie made a motion with her cigarette. "I had a weak moment. I needed money. Money to get Tom out of jail. He may be an ass, but I couldn't leave him in there. Anyway, it doesn't matter. I'm not angry with you."

"Have you seen Krista?"

"Krista?"

"Yes, my neighbor, the young girl who joined us at Café Einstein that night we all went out. She's missing. She's . . . I don't know. I'm worried."

"No, I haven't. Honestly, I haven't seen her since that night."

"Maggie, maybe you should go home with your mother. For a while."

"Aren't you going to introduce us to your Tante?" Said the girl lying on some pillows next to Maggie. She was obviously American. The young man was nodded out, asleep. "You're the lady who lived in East Berlin your whole life? That is so cool!"

"Sorry," Maggie said. "Tante Eva, this is my friend Laura."

"I've heard all about you," said Laura. "You're the reason Maggie came to Berlin."

To think she was the reason. And yet, look at this mess. Was she the reason for this mess, too?

"Nice to meet you," Eva said. Her hands were shaking. She needed a pill, but she wouldn't take one now.

"Hans is downstairs waiting for me. I'm going away. I wanted to see you, if you were still here. I didn't know if you'd left with your mother. I think you should go home and I thought I'd tell you that, tell you how I feel. It's not too late, Maggie."

"My mother's coming again tomorrow." Maggie sat up, and wrapped her arms around her thin knees. Her pockmarked face, her green pallor, the cigarette—all this, and yet she was just a girl. She shivered a bit as she spoke. "I don't know what to do. I hate her."

"Stay here! Party with us," said Laura.

"I'm leaving now with Hans. I don't know when I'll be back. I'm glad I got to say goodbye."

"Hey, I might be here when you get back. Who knows. I don't know."

"Oh, Maggie, I hope not."

"That's not a nice thing to say, Tante Eva." She stood. Well, she was in better shape. High, yes. But not so poisoned as before.

"I say it because I failed you."

"Stop," Maggie said. "My problems are my own. I've said this to you already. They have nothing to do with you."

She hugged her niece. "Goodbye, Maggie. May God bless you and look after you."

Maggie pulled back and looked at her aunt, and her distant eyes focused for a minute. "It's like a big hug, heroin," she said. "It's not anyone's fault. It is what it is. It's my . . ." She paused, then wrapped her arms around herself, swaying side to side. "It's my hug." Then Eva hugged her again, feeling her own big flesh wrap around her thin, shaky niece. Close to her ear, she said, "*Nein, meine liebe*, this is a hug." Then she kissed her niece on her head.

Maggie looked up at Eva but said nothing. But she had heard; she had heard her through her drugged-out mind.

Then Eva left, without looking back.

. . .

Hansi started the car as she walked back to it. Eva got in, slammed the door shut. He said, "As high as she is and she can still hold down her job. *Diese madchen ist etwas besonderers.*"

CHAPTER 32

Eva had taken two sleeping pills and fallen into a dark, dreamless sleep in the car. When she woke, her head like cotton, it was almost dark and they were far from the city, near to the cabin, near to Poland, really. Hansi was smoking, the window slightly open. The air that came in was quite cold. She felt it against her face, a bit wet, like a trace of ice on her warm, sleep-filled skin.

"*Wir werden shon dar sein, neh?*" she asked, more to wake herself up than anything.

"*Ja, mein liebchen.*" He smiled at her. She was his Liebchen. His Schatzi. She was someone he loved and counted on. All this trouble, all the trouble in the world. And what else can we ask of God than for one person to love us? Even if that person is as flawed as the bible says we all are.

"I made a stop, but you did not wake up. You are very tired today, no?"

"I'm waking up now. I am."

The countryside was beautiful in its emptiness. She opened a window wide for a moment and the air made her gasp. Endless snow-covered fields, dark mounds of hills beyond them, and a road that stretched out ahead. Occasionally they passed a small house or shed. Then there was the turn onto the last stretch of road, this one dirt and gravel, and ahead, the cabin.

"Did you meet Tom and Maggie before that day at my apartment?" she asked.

"And if I did?"

"Then it means Elena introduced you to them."

"Why these questions, Schatzi? It's over now. Things didn't work out as planned with Tom. But I still made a lot of money." He turned to her and grinned.

"But Elena? She always warned me against you."

Hansi started to laugh. He began laughing so hard he couldn't drive, so he pulled over.

"You laugh at me?" She wanted to hit him. "Me? Who loves you? Who is always there for you?"

"*Schatzi! Bist dumit mich nicht bose sein!* I only laugh because you are so naive. But you aren't really, are you? And I'm not laughing at you, really; I'm laughing at Elena. She is something else, warning you against me. How do you think I got your smells, eh? When she joined the Party, she was a schoolgirl, but we had lots of children working for us. She warned you against me? It's funny, it's just too funny."

Eva looked ahead. She saw the cabin at the end of the road. "My own daughter."

"We are all on the same side, Liebchen. You can't hold anything against her. It was the way things were then."

. . .

Hansi carried large, dark cases slowly from the car. They were very heavy looking, very different from what Eva had seen him bring in before. He didn't ask her to help, even though he was clearly struggling. He had parked the car right near the boat-house. At first Eva watched from the car; then she went into the cabin. It was very cold. She put together a fire and found a broom to sweep the dust that had collected since they'd last been there. She carried the wool blankets outside and shook them out. Lastly, she boiled some water for coffee.

"Ach, meine ruck tut mir weh," Hans said, holding his back and grimacing.

"Here, have a coffee." Eva passed him a hot mug. Her Hansi. What trouble had he really caused? Could she blame him for Maggie's problems? She was already using drugs before she came to Berlin. And yet.

Hans's face was quite red from exerting himself. He blew on his coffee, wiped his brow.

"Warum liebst du mich?" Eva asked.

"Warum?" Hansi laughed. "Women. You are all so crazy."

"Aber du liebst mich, doch?"

"Of course I love you."

"Warum? Warum mich?"

Hansi stood up, stretched his back. Then he came to her, and carefully wrapped his hands around her face. *"Du bist meine sicher Berliner, Ost Berliner. Paula war nicht wie du, ist nicht wie du. Ja, Die hat in der DDR gewohnt.* But you, your heart is like mine. Your heart is here in Berlin; Paula's is not. *Und was mehr? Ach*, woman, I don't know. It is love. It doesn't make any sense. You must know that by now."

This moment of tenderness startled Eva, but there was no reason to be startled. Ten years they had. Despite her regrets, regrets that grew and deepened. Having regrets didn't make her a bad person. Loving a man perhaps she wished she'd never loved. To endure regardless of regret, well that was the human condition, no? She closed her eyes and smelled the cigarettes from his hands, the sour smell of his sweat. She was a man's woman, and she'd always been. Despite her love for Liezel, or Elena, or Maggie. She loved her sister and her daughter, because they let her be a wife, a mother to a man's children, first her father's, then her Hugo's. They let her be the woman of the house, the woman in a man's house. And Maggie? She did love her, but what good did that do? Not much. And that was it, too: loving the women in her life never amounted to anything good. But now she was being ungrateful, the very trait that poisoned so many, that poisoned Maggie. Ingratitude. Her eyes still closed, she said a prayer. "Thank you, God, for my daughter, my sister, my niece. Look after them, guide them, care for them. And forgive me, God, for the truth in my heart, for the love I have for this man is stronger than it should be. Forgive me."

Hans embraced her; she put her head on his shoulder, inhaled him, his tart sweat, his smoky skin. Then she pulled back and stared into his eyes. It's fitting, she thought, that the last thing we see before we die is the thing we love, is the thing that kills us. A needle, a criminal, a man, a love. Love. Is it God's will? Is it the Devil's? Is it the two, working together?

Hans moved away, poked at the fire, then looked through the closet.

"I'm going on a walk," Eva said.

"*So spat?*"

"*Nicht für lange.*"

Eva pulled on a coat and stepped into Hans's rubber boots.

"Woman, you are taking my boots?"

"*Ja.* I need some air after that long ride. But I won't be gone long. You drink your coffee. Smoke a cigarette and I'll be back."

The moon shone over the lake now, so brightly she could see everything. The grooves in the frozen lake, the grooves in the frost, like a knife had run through it, and the sparks of snow that gathered along parts of the ice. She could see so well, until she got to the path in the surrounding woods. Then her eyes had to adjust again. The roots of the trees started to take shape in the dark and a focus came over her; her eyes felt keen, it was as if she were on a different planet, a different plane of existence. "I will die someday, God. And what will you do with me? Will I see Hugo, Mutti, Vati? Will I see Maggie there, sooner than she should be?" If life was to be lived to ensure a happy eternity, one must fight evil at all times, fight temptation. "Lead me not into temptation." Well, that was not what she really meant. The prayer was hollow and it filled her heart with grief. "Forgive me." Yes, that is what she really meant. If we can't be honest with our own souls, in our own private talks with God, then what? Then what?

The boathouse lay ahead, and in the clearing, it was lit brightly by the moon. Suddenly, she was very excited. She tripped in the boots and hurt her knee, hurt the palms of her hands trying to break her fall. She opened the broken door. The lockers were gone, but the rowboats were still there. And there were containers like the ones that Hans had moved into the cellar that night.

And then he was there. He wore a heavy coat and his soft-soled shoes; he'd made no noise.

"*Ach*, my feet are so wet. You! *Was willst du hier, Schatzi?*"

"I want to know you."

She was not afraid. But she felt lightheaded. She walked to one of the containers.

"Why can't you leave some things alone, Schatzi?"

"Don't hide things from me."

He walked past her and gruffly pushed her aside and opened one of the long containers, a case similar to one that a musician friend of Hugo's had used to carry around his large horn. Inside were guns.

"Do you know how rich I will be? It will change everything. And this is not illegal. *Wirklich.*"

"I see."

"No more drugs. No more of that." Hans closed the case. "Because of you."

"Because of me?"

"Yes. Well, and maybe for other reasons, too."

Say it. She wanted to ask him to say it. Her niece, whom she was supposed to protect. And Krista? She was gone. It was just one more failure in her life, a life that changed and changed and then would end.

"They are Kalashnikovs. I got them at such a good price. The Cold War is over now, Schatzi. These guns are flooding the market, but the demand is still high. And I have buyers in Serbia, and in the Middle East. I keep some here, for me. But with my partner, we have a warehouse filled to the ceiling with these."

Eva reached out to touch one.

"Here," Hans said. He picked one up and handed it to her. She dropped it, then picked it up, found a way to hold it. She cradled it in her arms awkwardly. And he leaned toward her again, now that her hands were full, and cupped her face there in the dark cabin. *"Für dich. Alles für dich."*

"How bad are you?"

"I'm not bad. I am the one who looks after you. This is all legal! When I sell these, I am buying you a proper apartment. I'll spend a lot of time here in Berlin. I won't always be in Poland. You'll see."

Eva hoisted the gun around and pointed it Hans.

"It's not loaded."

"*Ich weiss.*"

"I'm not a bad man."

"I am more worried about my soul than yours, Hansi."

"Put the gun down."

Eva put the gun down. Hansi reached over and closed the box. "Let's go. Come, Schatzi. Let's go back."

He led the way in front of her, and for some reason that made it harder than when she had come out here alone. She held on to his back, a shaky hand on his thick shoulder.

"Schatzi," he said, not turning back to look at her while he spoke, but continuing to lead the way. "It is the beginning of a new world, a better world. I will take you with me. I will show you the way."

ACKNOWLEDGMENTS

Thank you Marya, Mark, Steven, Jessica, Jack, Thelma, and Greywood Arts for all your amazing help in making this book happen.